Rough Around the Edges MEETS Refined

Rough Around the Edges MEETS Refined

RACHAEL ANDERSON
USA TODAY BESTSELLING AUTHOR

HEA PUBLISHING

This is a work of fiction. The characters, names, incidents, places, and dialogue are products of the author's imagination, and are not to be construed as real. The opinions and views expressed herein belong solely to the author and do not necessarily represent the opinions or views of HEA Publishing, LLC. Permission for the use of sources, graphics, and photos is also solely the responsibility of the author.

ISBN: 978-1-941363-09-6

Published by HEA Publishing

For Cassie. You are darling.

One

Seven Months Earlier

A RED ROSE landed on the top of the closed mahogany casket. Cassie didn't know who had thrown it. She simply watched as it slid to the left then stopped, its long stem hanging precariously over the edge. She hadn't thought to bring flowers—only the two halves of a geode that had rested on the sleek, black shelf in her family room. They felt rough and hard against her palms, as though they, too, would rather be anywhere but here. She slowly bent down and placed them on the top of the casket.

They didn't move or slide like the flower had. They just sat there with the crystallized insides winking up at her. She quickly retracted her fingers and took two steps back, unable to look away from them.

The day Landon had proposed, he'd given Cassie a small gift box. Surrounded by his family and friends, her fingers shook as she'd opened it, only to find an ugly gray rock inside rather than the hoped for ring. It had been the equivalent of getting a lump of coal in her stocking for Christmas.

With a deep chuckle, Landon had taken the rock from her and tapped it against his parents' outdoor fireplace like he was cracking an egg. Two quick flicks of his wrist, and it had split open in a clean break, revealing an inside covered in light blue crystals. Resting against the beautiful backdrop was a large diamond ring.

Cassie had gasped, her fingers flying to cover her mouth.

"This geode symbolizes us," he'd said. "This part is you; this part is me. Together, we make a whole." Then he'd knelt down, holding out the half that contained the ring. "Say you'll be my other half, Cassidy Ellis. My better half."

Her heart had become a puddle at her feet, tears stung her eyes, and all she could do was nod. A grin split Landon's face, and he quickly slid the ring onto her shaking finger before jumping to his feet and drawing her into a kiss that made one of those spinning rides at an amusement park seem tame. Whistles and applause echoed around them, beating in her ears like a powerful bass drum.

Normally, Cassie wasn't one to seek the limelight, but in that blissful moment, life had never felt more perfect. She was marrying the man of her dreams—the man of most girls' dreams. Landon was handsome, intelligent, suave, and wealthy. He was prince charming, offering her the promise of a happily ever after.

But, as things turned out, it was the promised "happily ever after" that was the fairytale. Not her life.

How naïve she'd been back then.

"Oh, sweetie, my heart hurts for you." Cassie's mother's well-padded arms squeezed her tightly from the side. "Are you sure you don't want me to stay with you tonight?"

"I'll be fine, Mom." Cassie returned the embrace half-heartedly, unable to pry her gaze away from the casket. At the young age of twenty-four, Cassie was a widow.

"You shouldn't be alone right now," her mother insisted. "I'm worried about you."

Cassie blinked, trying to feel something, anything. But her heart felt like that geode. Hard on the outside and hollow within. The only difference was that when cracked, her heart didn't have any pretty crystals inside. It was just . . . empty.

"I really think I should stay." The finality of her mother's words made Cassie snap out of it.

"No. Really, I'm fine. I just need to be alone right now, that's all." More than anything, Cassie wanted this day to be put to rest with Landon's body. She was tired of playing the part of the grieving widow when she wasn't grieving at all.

Her mother still looked hesitant. "If you're sure."

"I'm sure."

"At least let me drive you home. Dad can drop your car off later."

Cassie shook her head. "There's something I need to do first, and I need to do it alone." No one else would understand her errand, and she wasn't ready to make them understand. "Please. You go home with Dad, and tell everyone thanks for coming. I promise I'll call you tomorrow." It was an empty promise, and they both knew it. Cassie simply wanted the phone calls and condolences to go away.

A tear eased from the corner of her mother's eye, but she nodded anyway, gave Cassie a squeeze, and rejoined her husband.

Several yards away, her father nodded in parting, her two sisters and their husbands offered sympathetic and tentative waves, and her brothers and their wives watched with pity-filled eyes. Nearly her entire family had come to offer their support—from a distance. Always from a distance.

She let her gaze linger on her family briefly before she turned back and met the cold, hard stare of Landon's mother. Her steel blue eyes were filled with accusation. Cassie was the undeserving girl who'd stolen her prized son, ruined a marriage, and now look what had happened. It didn't matter that Landon had made the choice to drink and drive. It didn't matter that he'd nearly killed a young girl in that accident. In his mother's mind, Cassie had driven him to it.

Their gazes locked, and for a moment, it felt like a stand-off. Which one of them had loved Landon the most? Who would stay at his graveside the longest?

You win, Cassie thought. *Hands down, you win.* She adjusted the strap of her purse, gave the coffin one last glance, and turned away. Her feet stumbled as she crossed the uneven grass in the uncomfortable three-inch heels, with her dark pencil skirt hugging her knees together. They were clothes that Landon had picked out. It had been her final show of respect to a man she didn't respect at all. The Colorado summer sun heated her neck as, one step at a time, she walked away from one life and toward another. Her white sedan came into view, and Cassie focused on that. Ten steps . . . seven . . . five . . . three, two, one.

She yanked the door open and slid inside. Her hands refused to stop shaking as she started the engine.

Goodbye Landon, she thought as she tugged the black scarf from her neck, shrugged out of the tailored black jacket, and tossed her heels in the back.

Goodbye.

Two

Present Day

IN HIS DRIVEWAY, Noah killed the engine of his battered and beaten brownish Ford truck and studied the hand painted "Happy Birthday, Adelynn!" banner stretched across his front porch. Vines and flowers wrapped around each letter of his daughter's name, and purple and turquoise crepe paper streamers draped from the sign, hiding the front porch and the family room window beyond. A small smile touched his lips at the sight. His sister had worked her artistic magic yet again. Adi was one lucky girl.

If only Noah had been there to see the look on his daughter's face when she'd jumped off the bus and found the surprise waiting for her. If only he'd been there to help Emma hang it up or make the cake or wrap the presents or prepare the dinner.

If only he still had a job.

The weight of responsibility squeezed Noah like a vise. He needed to shake this off, go inside, wrap his now nine-

5

year-old girl in his arms, and swing her around while wishing her the happiest of birthdays. He needed to make her smile, make her laugh, and make this a day she'd remember all year long.

And he *would* do it. He just needed a few minutes to regroup and remember all the good things in his life. He still had his two beautiful, spirited daughters. He had Emma and Kevin next door, and Becky and Justin across the street, with Sam not too far away. And he had the rest of his life before him, just waiting to be figured out.

As his mother had once wisely told him, "Only after the rain comes the rainbows." Right now, his life was raining. Not pouring, just raining. All Noah needed to do was wait it out—maybe even dance with his daughters in it.

With a sigh, he pulled his keys from the ignition and opened the door to the frigid January weather. His breath fogged the air around him as he made his way across his newly shoveled driveway—Kevin's doing, no doubt—and toward his house. He pushed the front door open and spied his two girls at the bar, swiping their little fingers across the back of a turquoise, Barbie doll cake. Noah grinned, knowing exactly what his sister would say if she caught the little snitches.

"Hey," he called out. "There's a sign out there that says it's somebody's birthday. Which of my girls seems to think she's another year older?"

"Daddy!" they both cried, sucking the frosting off their fingers as they raced toward him, faces glowing. They threw their arms around his waist, and Noah suddenly found it easy to forget his troubles. Life was still really good.

"It's *my* birthday, silly!" Adi's dimples appeared as she smiled up at him. She tugged on Noah's fingers. "Come look. Aunt Emma made a ballerina cake with turquoise frosting, and Uncle Kevin is making my favorite dinner ever—hamburgers!"

"I helped," Kajsa interjected with a pout.

"And Kajsa helped," added Adelynn.

"I can see you're also helping yourselves to the cake," Noah pointed out.

They both had the grace to look sheepish. "We did it for you," blurted Kajsa.

"Me?"

"Yeah. We were just . . . making sure it doesn't taste awful."

Noah chuckled and grabbed them each around the waist, lifting them off the floor and tipping them upside down. "I thought I told you both that you're not allowed to have any more birthdays. No more cake, no more presents, and no more getting older. I forbid it."

The girls were giggling when Emma came in from the backyard, bringing with her a draft of chilled air and a plate of steaming hamburger patties. She wore a white baseball shirt with red sleeves. A circular sports logo decorated the front. Noah only noticed because it wasn't her usual style, and yet it looked good on her. It had probably been a gift from her sports-loving husband—one of his favorite teams or something. Kevin followed her in and untied his apron, wearing a similar shirt.

When Noah had first moved in, a wall separated the kitchen from the front room. But Emma had made him tear it down and replace it with a bar so the space would feel larger and more open. Now here they were, over three years later, and Noah still admired their handiwork. He loved renovating, building, and creating. He loved change—at least when it came to houses. When it came to jobs, he could do with a little more consistency.

"Well, look who finally came," Emma teased. "Your timing is impeccable, bro, as usual. Always showing up after the work is done. Ever heard the story of *The Little Red Hen*?"

"Ever heard the story of the Good Samaritan?" he countered.

Emma rolled her eyes while Kevin chuckled, throwing his apron over a chair. He kissed his wife on the forehead and said, "He got you there," before stealing the plate of patties and setting them on the table.

The front door burst open, revealing their shivering neighbor, Becky, and her husband, Justin.

"Brrr, it's cold out there," said Becky. "You should have asked for warmer weather for your birthday, Adi."

"You got that right." Kevin draped an arm around his wife, pulling her close. "Adi insisted on grilling hamburgers. Though with Emma's reputation for burning things, it's no wonder."

Emma elbowed him in the stomach, making him grunt. "Will you stop saying that? I only burn like ten percent of the things I cook."

"Not great odds when you want your birthday dinner to be perfect, right Adi?"

She giggled and nodded in response, and Kevin received another elbow to the gut.

"I didn't burn her cake," Emma defended.

"I don't know, did you? It was covered with frosting by the time I saw it. Is the cake burned, Kajsa?"

Kajsa shook her head. "Aunt Emma set the timer." This made everyone laugh, with the exception of Emma, who directed a scowl at Kajsa.

Becky held up a bowl as she made her way toward the kitchen. "The chips and potato salad are here, along with the world's best present. If the burgers are ready, let's get this party started."

"Yay!" Adelynn and Kajsa darted to the table, nearly knocking over two chairs in their haste.

"Girls, careful," Emma chided, but Noah only grinned. He didn't mind their excitement. They lived life the way it should be lived—with gusto.

They all settled around the table, prayed, and dug in. The burgers tasted wonderful—the way they always did when Kevin cooked. For the millionth time, Noah thanked his lucky stars that his sister and brother-in-law lived next door. He couldn't imagine coping as a single father without their help. Emma was always there if the girls needed something during the day, and Kevin was like a second father to them. And if that wasn't enough, Becky could always be counted on to swoop in and save the day if needed. Even though Noah missed the companionship he'd once shared with his late wife, he was never alone.

"Time for cake and presents!" Adelynn announced. Noah frowned at his half-eaten burger before he glanced at Adelynn's plate. She'd only taken about one bite of everything.

He shook his head. "Not gonna fly, Adi. You need to take at least two bites of everything before you get any cake."

Adelynn grabbed her burger and took another bite, then shoved in a spoonful of potato salad, followed by a chip. "There," she mumbled through a mouth full of food.

"Really?" Emma said dryly. "Two bites, and that's it? After all our hard work?"

"It's her birthday," said Noah.

"And if it wasn't her birthday, you'd still let her get away with it." Emma gave a small smile and shook her head. "You're such a pushover."

"And you're not?"

"I'm her aunt. I'm allowed."

Adelynn balanced the cake under two arms as she carried it carefully to the table. She looked so old and independent, like she was nine going on twenty. Noah wanted time to stop, or at least slow down. He wanted to keep his girls young and innocent for as long as he could.

Instead, he grabbed a lighter and lit the candles.

"Happy birthday to me," Adelynn started the song, and the others quickly joined in, singing faster than usual to keep up with the birthday girl. Before Noah could catch his breath, the candles had been blown out, and Adelynn was racing to the bar where all of her presents were on display.

"Can I open them, Daddy, please?" Her dark eyes were large. Happy. So beautiful. So impossible to say no to.

"Sure," he said.

She ripped into his presents first, squealing when she found the Barbie ballerina doll she'd been wanting, along with a Princess-opoly game, some new winter boots, and a turquoise sweater. "Thank you, Daddy! I love them," she said, throwing her arms around him. Emma and Kevin's gift came next—a new art set, the same gift they gave every birthday. The girls adored them. They both wanted to be artists like their Aunt Emma.

Before Adelynn could reach for the last gift, Becky snatched it up. "I need to explain something before you open it. This is a birthday gift for both you and Kajsa. We're just giving it to Kajsa a few months early because . . . well, you'll see." Becky waved Kajsa over to help open the gift, and the girls pulled out two pairs of black ballet-type shoes and some textured white socks. They stared at them in confusion.

"They're dance shoes and poodle socks," Becky explained. "Remember when I measured your feet a couple weeks ago?"

They nodded.

"This is why," Becky explained. "I signed you both up for four months of Irish dance lessons starting next Tuesday."

"I get to take dance?" Adelynn's eyes became large saucers of excitement. When Becky confirmed with a head nod, she jumped up and down. "I get to take dance! I get to take dance!"

Kajsa didn't look nearly as thrilled. "What's Irish dance?"

"It's sort of like clogging," explained Becky. "You have to learn to move your feet really fast, and there's skipping and jumping, and . . . I think you're going to love it. Especially the instructor. She was one of my clients a few months back, and she's so much fun."

Kajsa still didn't look convinced, which was exactly how Noah felt. He'd priced out dance lessons before—not Irish dance, but ballet—and knew it wasn't cheap. How much money had Becky paid for those lessons? And what if the girls loved it so much they wanted to continue? What then? He still had school loans to pay off, a house to maintain, and two girls to take care of.

And no job to pay for any of it.

"Becky . . ." Noah started to say. But as he watched a grinning Adelynn plop down and pull on the funny-looking socks, he couldn't find it in himself to argue.

Becky's hand covered his, and her voice sounded quiet in his ear. "A friend of mine teaches the class. She's giving me an awesome deal, and if your girls want to continue after this summer, she'll work something out that you can afford."

"I don't know," he said, allowing the worry of the future to creep back in.

"Haven't you learned by now that you can't argue with my wife?" Justin said, slipping his arm around the back of her chair and pulling her close.

"If you need help dropping them off or picking them up, I've got you covered," added Becky.

"It's not that. It's just . . ." Noah wasn't sure how to formulate his thoughts into words.

Becky's head cocked to the side, and she gave his hand a squeeze. "They need something other than school and family. They need opportunities to develop their talents. Just let them try this and see how it goes. Please?"

Noah glanced at Kajsa, who was back in her seat, staring at her new dance shoes with a bleak look that broke his heart. Unlike Adelynn, this wasn't what she wanted. But what she did want was something beyond all of their reach. Riding lessons made dance look cheap. Noah's heart constricted.

Why did Kajsa have to love horses so much? Why couldn't Noah be in a position to give her that dream? Why couldn't he be the one to give Adelynn this gift?

"Okay," he finally said to Becky. He'd let Adelynn have her lessons, and he'd encourage Kajsa to give it a try as well. And then he'd pray that Kajsa would come to love something else more than horses. Miracles do happen, right?

Emma's chair squeaked as she pushed it back. She grabbed her husband's hand and pulled him up as well. "We have one more present for everyone. And I can't believe that we actually have to announce it." She scowled at the group. "It's a good thing none of you are detectives because your observation skills are seriously lacking."

Noah shot Becky and Justin a glance. They looked as clueless as he did.

With a sigh, Emma turned Kevin around and pointed at the sports insignia on the back of his shirt. On closer inspection, it wasn't a sports logo. It was a circle with the words "Thing 1" scribbled inside it. Emma then pointed to the back of her shirt, where "Thing 2" was written inside another circle. Then she spun around and tugged on the bottom of her shirt, un-wrinkling the fabric. Noah had to squint to see the small cursive writing of "Thing 3 & Thing 4" written inside another circle.

An excited shriek sounded, a chair hit the ground, and Becky lunged at Emma and Kevin, hugging them both. "Are you serious? *Twins*?"

Emma nodded, her smile growing bigger with each passing second. Then Noah and Justin were out of their seats, hugging them as well. It was no secret that Emma and Kevin had been trying for a baby for years. And now they were getting twins.

Miracles really do happen.

Noah felt a tug on his hand, and he looked down to find Kajsa biting her lip in confusion. "What's happening?" she asked quietly.

Noah put his arm around her and gestured for Adelynn to join them. He crouched down to their level. "Guess what, princesses? Your Aunt Emma is going to have two babies."

"Two?" They both said.

He nodded.

Kajsa dropped her dancing shoes on the counter and threw her young arms around Emma's stomach. Adelynn joined her seconds later.

"Two babies!" cried Adelynn. "That means we won't have to share, Kajsa."

"Are they both girls?" said Kajsa.

"I don't know yet. We won't find that out for another month or so."

"When are you due?" Becky asked.

Kevin hugged Emma from behind, pulling her close. He rested his chin on the top of her head. "August, though they'll probably come in July."

"August! That's forever away," pouted Adelynn. Kajsa frowned at her dancing shoes again, probably wondering how many times she'd have to wear them before the twins came.

Noah couldn't help but laugh, and all the adults joined in, filling the room with the kind of feeling Noah had come to associate with this house. A deep sense of love, family, and hope.

If Emma and Kevin could get their miracle, maybe things would work out for him too.

Noah shut off the family room light, enshrouding himself in darkness. The tree in his front yard moved with the wind, creating an eerie shadow in the space. He dropped down on the couch and leaned forward, resting his chin on his palms. Exhaustion overtook his body, but with the state his mind was in, sleep wouldn't come easily. Sometimes, Noah envied how quickly his girls could drop off. But at the same time, he was grateful the worries of the world didn't rest on their little shoulders.

A soft knock on the front door interrupted his thoughts. Noah opened it to find Emma hugging her arms to her chest to ward off the cold. He quickly ushered her inside.

"This pregnancy must be getting to me already." She smiled. "I left my ring by the sink. Sorry. I hope I didn't wake you."

"Nope. Still wide awake. Let me grab it for you." Noah quickly retrieved the ring and handed it back to his sister. "It's a good thing you came back tonight or the girls might have found it in the morning. Who knows what would have happened to it then."

Emma nodded knowingly. "Nothing intentional, I'm sure. But Adi does love to try it on."

"Thanks for all your help tonight. I really appreciate all you do for the girls."

A soft smile formed. "They're my girls too. And you know I love it."

"I do."

She took a step toward the door then paused, studying Noah with a shrewd look. "Is something the matter?"

"Just tired. It's been a long day."

The moment her eyes narrowed, Noah knew he hadn't fooled her. She plopped down on the couch and patted the spot next to her. "It's more than that. I know you. Something's been bothering you all night, and I want to know what it is."

He should have known that Emma would see right through him. Sometimes her perceptiveness was annoying, and sometimes, like tonight, he could have hugged her for it. Noah sat down beside her and raked his fingers through his hair.

"I was let go today," he said quietly.

Her quick intake of breath signaled that she'd heard him. "Why?"

"Not enough business. It's the slow time of year for the construction industry, and they couldn't afford to keep paying me."

"But I thought they'd promised you a promotion after your graduation last month. I've been expecting to hear news of that."

Noah had too. He'd worked so hard to get his construction management degree, believing that things would look up when he did. Unfortunately, it hadn't worked out that way. "They can't promote someone they can't pay."

"Oh, Noah." Her hand covered his. "I'm so sorry."

He shrugged. "It'll be okay. I'll find something else. It's just . . . frustrating."

She squeezed his hand. "I'm here for you. You know that, right? Whatever you need, I'll always be here."

He gave her shoulder a playful nudge. "Until those babies come, you mean. Then you'll need to focus on your own family. Believe me, I've been there. Newborns are amazing and special, but they're a handful. Literally. I can only imagine what it will be like with two."

Emma looked him in the eye. "You're right. I'll be a wife and mother first, but always a sister and aunt second. I'm not going anywhere. And you'd better not either. I'm going to need you and the girls when these little angels come."

"We'll be here." Where else would they be?

"It's settled then," Emma said matter-of-factly. "Life will be crazy for a while, but we'll muddle through it, and Kajsa and Adelynn will make the best babysitters ever. My two babies are going to be the luckiest girls alive."

A weight eased off his chest, and Noah smiled. "Girls, huh? Has Kevin heard you say that?"

"He says they have to be boys. We have enough estrogen in the family already. But I keep telling him a mother's intuition is never wrong."

15

Noah leaned back, draping his arm across the back of the couch. "I have to agree about the estrogen. Kajsa and Adi have more than enough to go around. The thought of them becoming teenagers scares me to death."

Instead of laughing or teasing him, Emma's brow furrowed. She chewed on her lower lip the way she did when she wanted to say something but wasn't sure she should.

"What is it?" Noah said.

She worried her lower lip a bit longer. "It's just that . . . well, Angie's been gone for four years now. I'm just wondering if . . . you know . . . you have any desire to date again."

Noah sighed. "Not you too, Emma." Becky was already on his case. As a real estate agent, she came across a lot of available women, and ever since Noah had moved here, she'd been subtly trying to set him up with all of them.

"Becky told me she's been trying to nudge you back into the dating scene."

"Shove me is more like it."

A light chuckle sounded. "She's right, though. It's time. And not just for you. Adelynn and Kajsa—"

"Have you, Becky, and Sam."

"Of course they do. But like you said, I have twins coming, Becky's getting busier and busier with her real estate stuff, and Sam is away at college now, preparing to start her own life."

Noah scowled. The moment Emma and Kevin had announced the twins, he'd known things would be different. Change was always inevitable, and Noah would deal with it as it came. The twins would arrive, Kevin and Emma would get sucked into their new role as parents, and he, Adelynn, and Kajsa would adapt. That was how life worked.

"I'm not saying you should run out and marry the first girl that comes along," Emma continued. "I'm saying you should stop running away from it."

"I'm not running away."

Emma's sudden burst of laughter jarred Noah. "You're joking, right? The next time Becky mentions a woman she wants you to meet, do me a favor and go look in the mirror. You'll see pure, raw terror."

"Give me a break."

"I'm serious. You are most definitely running."

Noah shifted, feeling uncomfortable. Maybe she was right. Maybe he was, but why was that a bad thing? Instead of spending time, money, and effort dating, he'd been focused on finishing his degree, taking care of his girls, and being the best father he knew how to be. Wasn't that enough? Wasn't *he* enough? Even when Angie was alive, she'd been so busy with school and work that Noah had been the one to cook the girls' dinner, kiss their ouchies, and read them bedtime stories. Why couldn't he continue to do that?

"You can fall in love more than once, you know," said Emma quietly. She gave his fingers a gentle squeeze. "I've seen the way you look at me and Kevin sometimes. Or Becky and Justin. I see the loneliness in your eyes."

Noah pulled his hand free and clenched it. "Of course I get lonely. Some days I miss Angie so much I'd give anything to get her back. But that's what happens when someone you love dies. You miss them. It's called life."

"It's also part of life to let go, move on, and discover that you can open your heart to someone new."

"Is that what you'd do if something happened to Kevin?" Noah shouldn't have said it, but Emma had no idea what she was talking about. What she was asking. "You don't just let go of someone you love and decide to move on. It doesn't work like that. Those memories will always be there, making me smile sometimes or squeezing my chest so much I can barely breathe others. I can't push that aside and walk into another relationship. Right now, Adi and Kajsa are enough for me, and I have no desire to fall in love again. Ever."

Noah clamped his mouth shut, feeling the familiar

constriction in his chest. He hated constriction. Why couldn't he talk about Angie without this response? Why couldn't he do what Becky and Emma seemed to think he was capable of doing and let go?

Emma's hand found his again, and this time she gripped it hard. "I'm sorry, Noah. You're right. I don't know what it feels like. I just miss seeing you happy, that's all."

"I am happy." Noah stood, signaling an end to the conversation. Emma took her cue, gave him a kiss on the cheek, and left. Through the front window, he watched her pick her way across the snow then smile when she saw Kevin coming to look for her. Hand-in-hand, they walked back home.

Yes, Noah did get lonely. But he *was* happy. He had a nice home, two beautiful daughters, a college degree, and the prospect of a new and exciting job just around the corner.

That was all he needed.

Three

RIGHT CROSS OVER, hop up, hop back two-three-four." With her rigid back to her class, Cassie slowly walked them through each step. Then she spun around and clasped her fingers together. "Now I want you to try." She repeated the steps and watched each girl in her class of eight. As usual, Adelynn, Lizzie, Kara, and Hailey picked it right up. Three others were almost there. And then there was Kajsa, the sweet girl with two left feet who never complained but never seemed to find much enjoyment in dancing either. Not for the first time, Cassie wondered why Becky had signed her up.

"No, Kajsa, that's not right. It goes like this." Adelynn executed an almost flawless hop back two-three-four before raising her blond eyebrow expectantly.

Kajsa tried, but stumbled and took five steps instead of four, ending with her weight on the wrong foot. Cassie smiled and intervened. "Let's try it again, only more slowly this time." Four attempts later, Kajsa finally pulled it off. Cassie was quick to congratulate her, but Kajsa ducked her head against the praise, looking embarrassed that she'd taken so much longer than the others to learn the steps. Cassie's heart went out to her.

"All right, girls, time for our cool down."

They all grumbled but sank to the floor anyway, bending forward to touch their toes in a stretch. After only four lessons, they had this part of the routine down pat, and it was adorable to watch them attempt to keep their legs straight.

Five minutes later, parents started to arrive. One after another, the girls thanked Miss Cassie and skipped out the door. Their faces were bright with excitement as they met their mom or dad and gushed about class and what they'd learned, just like they always did. It was one of Cassie's greatest rewards for teaching. The only exception was Kajsa, who always met Becky with a resigned expression.

Today, however, there was no Becky to greet them, even after all the other girls had left. There was no one. Cassie glanced out the window. Maybe she'd lost track of time and had forgotten. Cassie pulled out her phone to call her friend when an ugly brown, beat-up truck sped into the lot, scattering some of the snow that had accumulated during the past hour. It slid to a crooked halt in front of the glass doors that led into the dance studio.

Both girls cried out, "It's Daddy!" and rushed for the door. It was the happiest Cassie had ever seen Kajsa.

Curious, she studied the man who jumped from the truck, clearly frantic about being late. He had short, wavy dark blond hair and the most striking blue eyes Cassie had ever seen. His rumpled t-shirt was filthy and his jeans were covered in holes and what appeared to be paint. But the girls didn't seem to care as they flung their little arms around him.

So that was Noah Mackie.

Becky had told Cassie about the single father who lived across the street from her. Well, *gushed* would be more accurate. According to her friend, not only was he handsome, but he was incredibly talented, the best father in the world, funny, kind, and . . . had Becky mentioned handsome? She couldn't have been more obvious.

Unfortunately, Cassie's interest in Noah Mackie went only as far as his two daughters. If Becky wanted to sign the girls up for her Irish dancing class, awesome. If her friend was out to set her up with some guy—no thanks. For Cassie, marriage was a been there, done that sort of thing—not a rinse and repeat.

Thankfully, Becky had dropped the subject of Noah and signed his two girls up for dance instead.

And now here he was, helping them into his truck. Cassie was glad they'd run out to meet him so she didn't have to make polite, uncomfortable small talk.

With a sigh, Cassie spun around and began cleaning up the foyer. She bent to grab a sweatshirt that had been left behind by one of her young dancers and shook it out, immediately recognizing it as Kajsa's. A horse galloped across the front of it, looking ready to rush the world head-on.

The door opened behind her and a whoosh of winter air swept around her. "I think my daughter left her sweatshirt."

She forced a smile as she turned around, holding up the sweatshirt. "You mean this one?"

"That would be the one." He took it from her then held out a hand covered in white paint splotches for her to shake. "You must be Cassie. I'm Noah Mackie."

Cassie stared at the painter's hand, unsure of what to do. If he was just any father, it wouldn't have been a big deal. Paint or no paint, she'd shake it, smile, and tell him it was nice to meet him as well. But he was not just any father. He was the single, incredibly good-looking man that Becky had wanted her to meet—possibly even date and who knows what else. That made him a man Cassie didn't want to touch or get to know. Had Becky pressured him into meeting her as well? Was he here to check Cassie out as a potential date, or was he really only searching for a mislaid sweatshirt?

The silence turned awkward, and Noah finally dropped his hand. "Sorry. I forgot about the paint. Normally, I wash up after a job, but I was running late. Which is something I'm also sorry about—being late, that is. I'm not normally a flake."

She waved off the apology. "No worries. Parents sometimes get held up. I understand." Cassie wasn't about to explain why she hadn't taken his hand before. He'd have to chalk it up to her being a priss or whatever. Which was fine. He didn't seem like the type who would like high-maintenance girls, so maybe that opinion would nip whatever seed Becky might have planted in the bud.

Noah shuffled his feet, glanced out the door toward his car, then back at Cassie. "Well, it's, uh . . . good to finally meet you. The girls really like your class. They're always going on and on about how much fun they're having."

Cassie lifted an eyebrow. "Even Kajsa?"

"Uh . . ." He laughed. "Okay, so maybe not Kajsa. She comes because Becky gifted her the lessons and she doesn't want to be ungrateful. I hope she doesn't give you a hard time."

"Not at all. She's very polite and tries her best. She's just not . . . as enthusiastic about it as the others."

"That doesn't surprise me. She's a bit of a tomboy, so this really isn't her scene. Becky's hoping she'll come to love it, but I don't think it's going to happen. Kajsa's never been the dress-up, put-on-a-performance type of girl. She'd rather run out in the rain without her umbrella and splash in the puddles. But she doesn't complain about coming either, so, who knows, maybe you can change her mind." His words ended on a hopeful note.

Cassie hesitated. What did that mean? Was Noah the type of father who tried to push his daughters to be something they weren't? Or was this his "fun sense of humor" that Becky had referenced?

"Yeah. Maybe," she finally said.

22

More silence.

His feet shuffled again, and Noah nodded toward the door. "Well, I guess I'd better get the girls home. It was good to finally meet you. I'm nearly finished with a project I've been working on, so you'll probably be seeing more of me and less of Becky."

"Good to know." Cassie was relieved that the awkward conversation was at an end. Another whoosh of cold air flew into the room as he left, and she resumed her efforts to tidy the foyer area. Then she pulled her keys from her purse and stared out into the darkening night. It had been snowing all day, which would mean her twenty-minute commute home would probably take more like forty minutes.

Cassie glanced back at the old, ratty carpet covering the floor of the foyer. Through the too-small glass window into the dance studio, she noticed the scuffed floor was in need of a refinishing, the walls in need of a fresh coat of paint, and the space in need of another fifty square feet.

Two more parents had contacted her yesterday about signing their kids up for dance, and Cassie was running out of space. Maybe it was time to stop reworking her basement plans and hand them over to someone who could do something about them.

Noah opened his front door to find a shivering Becky carrying a steaming pot of something. Yesterday and the day before, it had been Emma bringing dinner.

He stepped back, allowing her to come inside. "What did you and Emma do, make dinner assignments? She pulled the short stick for Monday and Tuesday which left you with Wednesday?"

Becky brushed past him and headed for the kitchen. "No idea what you're talking about." She set the pan down on the counter with a light clang and smiled up at him. "I tried a new recipe for cheesy broccoli soup tonight and made way too much. I didn't want it to go to waste."

"That's funny." Noah lifted the lid, felt the steam hit his face, and breathed in an aroma that made his stomach grovel for a taste. "Emma said the same thing on Monday when she brought us lasagna. And wouldn't you know, yesterday chicken was on sale and she didn't have room in her freezer, so she *had* to make extra."

"That's not funny," said Becky, her poker face still intact. "Sounds to me like you're surrounded by nitwits."

"No." Noah replaced the lid and gave her a side hug. "I'm surrounded by angels. Thanks, Beck. But you've already done more than enough by recommending me to some of your clients. It's because of you that I've got work. You don't need to make us dinner too. Though I have to admit, that soup smells incredible."

"Tastes good, too." Her eyes twinkled. "And where are my girls? How was dance today?"

"Showering." Noah grimaced. "You should have smelled my truck after I picked them up. I'm thinking it's time to invest in some deodorant."

Becky leaned a hip against the counter and folded her arms. "They're growing up. Before you know it, they're going to follow in Sam's footsteps and take off for college."

"Now there's a happy thought," Noah said dryly, making her laugh.

"So . . ." she hedged. "Did you get a chance to meet Cassie when you picked them up?" To most people, the question would have sounded so innocent. But after all of her hints about how Cassie was single, and pretty, and talented, and a wonderful person, and *single,* Noah knew better.

"I did," he said, and left it at that. He wasn't about to tell Becky that her friend was the most standoffish person he'd ever met. Cassie's expression had been too serene, her posture too perfect, and her sense of humor too nonexistent. She wouldn't even shake his hand. There was no denying she was beautiful, but if Noah was actually looking—which he wasn't—it would be for more than a pretty face. He'd want someone who knew how to have fun; someone who could be a wonderful mom to his girls. Cassie didn't seem to fit that description.

Becky wasn't about to let it drop. "And . . . ?" she prompted.

"And what?"

She rolled her eyes. "What did you think?"

"Uh . . . she seems nice." Sort of.

"Nice?" Becky said. "That's it? Really?"

"We talked for a total of five minutes. And yeah, she was nice." Sort of.

"Did you think she was pretty?"

"Sure."

"Intelligent?"

Noah was ready to end the conversation and eat the soup. "Like I said, five minutes."

Becky frowned. "I can't believe you only talked to her for five minutes. You should have given it at least fifteen."

"And let the girls smell up my cab even more? I don't think so."

Becky leveled him a hard stare. "Just promise me the next time you're able to pick them up, you'll give her a chance."

He sighed. Becky had done so much for him and the girls, and he would bend over backwards to return all the favors. But this? This made him incredibly uncomfortable. If he was going to meet a girl, he wanted to do it on his own terms and in his own way—not be pushed into something that wouldn't have a chance of going anywhere but down.

"I don't know," he finally said. "She doesn't really seem like my type."

"Wow, that's pretty amazing you could know that after only *five minutes*," Becky said.

25

"Hey, sometimes that's all it takes."

"And most of the time, it takes a lot longer." She paused, and Noah could almost see her mind thinking and calculating. "Promise me one thing, will you?"

It was on the tip of Noah's tongue to say "not a chance," but after all she'd done for him, Noah couldn't force the words out. "Depends. What is it?"

"Find out what her favorite flavor of ice cream is."

That sounded easy. Too easy. What was Becky up to? "If I do, will you stop trying to set me up?"

"With her? Sure."

"I mean period. I mean it, Beck. I do this for you, and you have to promise there will be no more matchmaking attempts."

From the way her brow furrowed, Becky didn't much care for that idea, but she finally nodded. "Fine. But you can't let Cassie brush you off with an I-don't-have-a-favorite-flavor excuse. She has to give you an answer."

"And if she really doesn't have a favorite flavor?"

"Who doesn't have a favorite flavor?" Becky gave him a triumphant grin. "I've got to run now. Be sure to tell the girls hi for me."

"Thanks again for the soup."

Hunger forgotten, Noah watched the door close behind his neighbor. He drew his bottom lip into his mouth and bit down on it, thinking that he should be the one wearing the triumphant grin. One simple question and Becky would stop her matchmaking efforts for good. No sweat.

Why, then, did Noah suddenly feel as though he'd walked into some sort of carefully laid trap?

Four

THE CONCRETE WAS cold and hard, and the air around Cassie not much warmer. She was sitting on the floor of her basement, leaning her head against the only wall that Landon had erected before his accident. The two-by-fours felt rough against her back, and the splinters pulled at the hair in her ponytail.

She looked from the graph paper on the ground to the unfinished basement that surrounded her. On paper, the design worked. It gave her an outside entrance for the girls and an inside entrance for her. It gave her a family room, a dance studio, and a bathroom. But would she like the end result? Was the bathroom big enough for the girls to change in? Would the foyer be too tight of a space for parents to wait? Would the studio get enough light? Would that extra corner of space look awkward? And would the extra little family room be as cozy and warm as she wanted?

How many times had she sketched out various floor plans? How many different configurations had she tried?

Enough to know that this was the one that would work the best. Right?

She frowned at the sketch.

What Cassie needed was another pair of eyes to look it over. For the first time since Landon's accident, she found herself missing her late husband. He'd always been the type to find the problems with anything, and right now, Cassie needed his critical way of thinking, even though she already knew he'd nix the plan as soon as he saw it. Landon had wanted to turn the basement into a man cave, not a dance studio. He'd wanted a pool table, a massive TV, a cold and slippery leather couch, and a small kitchenette. She'd tried to convince him there was space enough for both of them, but when they sat down to draw it all out, there wasn't. Not unless he could go without his pool table, which he'd been unwilling to do.

In the end, one of them had to sacrifice, and that person was Cassie. It was always Cassie. She had a perfectly good job at Hanson Imaging. Why did she want to be a dance instructor anyway? He'd asked the question so many times she'd lost count.

But now that Landon was gone, Cassie didn't have to sacrifice. She could do whatever she wanted.

And yet she still waffled.

Hmm . . . Was there something she'd missed? Something she hadn't thought of? Something she'd be kicking herself for not thinking of later? If only there was someone to call for a second opinion. Someone who'd done this before. Someone with a good eye. Someone like . . . Becky.

Feeling like she was grasping at straws, Cassie tugged her phone from her pocket and scanned through her small list of contacts to Becky's name. Before she could rethink anything, she placed the call. A quiet ringing sounded in her ear, followed by Becky's perky voice.

"Cass, this had better not be another one of your pocket calls. I can't take anymore disappointment."

"No such luck," said Cassie with a smile.

"I'm relieved to hear it."

Though Cassie hadn't known Becky for too long—she'd been the real estate agent who'd helped Cassie find her current dance space—Becky was the sort of person who became insta-friends with everyone. Or maybe Cassie had needed a friend so badly that she'd latched on to Becky the way a lost puppy would do to the first person who offered it food or showed kindness.

But Becky had never made her feel like a lost little puppy. It was why calling her was easy to do.

"I need a favor," said Cassie.

"Perfect. I like doing favors. What's up? Do you need my help sewing dance costumes? Answering phones? Redesigning that drab little studio I should have never shown you in the first place?"

"It was the only place I could afford."

"And I find that as sad now as I did then."

"Is that why you keep referring me to everyone you meet who has a daughter between the ages of six and eighteen?"

"No—at least not totally. I refer you because you're talented, a wonderful teacher, and who wouldn't want their kid to learn Irish dance? It's the coolest style of dance ever."

Cassie laughed. "Well, thank you regardless. Because of you, I now have some really great news."

A happy squeal sounded on the other end of the line. "Are you saying you can afford to move now? Yay! I'll start looking for new spaces right away."

"I, uh . . . already found a place." Cassie cringed when she said it, hating that this "favor" wouldn't include a commission for Becky.

"Really? Where?" There was no disappointment in Becky's voice, only curiosity.

"My basement."

A gasp, followed by what sounded like a clap. "Oh, Cass. That's perfect! I had no idea you even had a basement, let alone one that will be large enough for a studio."

"That's why I'm calling. I've been trying to draw up plans for months now and could really use a second pair of eyes."

"I do have two of them," Becky said, sounding delighted. "And I'd love to help. When can I come over?"

"Whenever you have the time. I'm not picky. I'm just grateful you're willing to help."

"As if I'd ever say no to you. Friday morning work?"

"It's perfect."

"Great. See ya then."

"Thanks, Becky." Cassie set her phone down on the concrete floor. The basement suddenly felt lighter and warmer—more hopeful, which was a foreign feeling for Cassie of late. But ever since she'd met Becky, parts of her life had started to look up and fall into place. She'd found a studio she could afford, registered more girls than she'd expected her first year, and now this. Sometimes, Cassie couldn't help but wonder if Becky was part angel.

Noah wasn't one to shove things to the back burner. If the swing in the backyard needed fixing, he fixed it. If his car was due for an oil change, he changed it. And if he promised a friend he'd do something, he followed through as soon as possible.

Which was exactly why he showed up at the dance studio ten minutes before the end of class. He had a question to ask, and he needed an answer today. Then it would be over and done. Exactly how he liked it.

Casting a glance through the small window, Noah saw

all the girls on the floor, legs stretched out in front of them, stretching to reach their toes. Adelynn and a few others could do it, but Kajsa had about four inches to go and didn't appear very pleased about it.

While the girls stretched, Cassie walked gracefully around the room, straightening a leg here, pressing lightly on a back there, and tucking a chin toward the knee. When she came to Kajsa, her lips twitched slightly before she schooled her features into a serene expression and knelt beside his daughter. She said something that wiped the frustration from Kajsa's face and replaced it with a smile.

Intrigued, Noah took a few steps closer. What had Cassie said? When it came to Kajsa's frustrations, Noah could never say the right thing. If he tried for sympathy, she rolled her eyes. If he tried to tease a smile out of her, she grew more frustrated and stomped away. But all Cassie had to do is whisper a few words, and, like magic, happy Kajsa was back.

Cassie's shiny, strawberry blond hair was pulled back into a tight bun, and her movements were slow and deliberate. She personified tranquility. Her hips swayed slightly as she walked from one girl to the next, and when she spoke, everyone paid attention, including Noah, who couldn't hear a word she said. It was obvious the girls respected her, liked her, looked up to her.

Adelynn raised her hand and asked a question. Cassie smiled and shook her head in the negative. All the girls—with the exception of Kajsa—rose to their knees, and with palms together scooted slightly forward, saying something that looked like *"Please?"*

Noah took another step closer, wondering what was going on. It was like watching a movie on mute without any subtitles. If only he could read lips.

She finally held out her hand in an okay-okay-you-win sort of gesture. Then she walked to the corner and fiddled with the stereo system. The faint, muffled strains of some folk-type music sounded, and Cassie walked regally back to the center front of the class. She straightened her arms at her side, turned her fists to the back of the room, raised her chin and waited a few beats before her legs and feet started moving faster than Noah had ever seen legs move. She flew through the steps fluidly, dancing around the room, then forward and backward, before she finally stopped at the front and executed a flawless bow.

The girls burst into applause—even Kajsa—and Cassie smiled. A dimple appeared in the side of her cheek, and her vibrant green eyes lit up. They contrasted nicely with her strawberry blond hair. In that moment, she looked lovely, talented, and approachable.

Maybe he'd misjudged her a little.

Soon, more parents arrived, and the class was dismissed. The moment Kajsa saw Noah through the open door, she yelled out, "Daddy!" and came charging his way. Adelynn soon followed. As the girls barreled into him, Noah's gaze caught Cassie's briefly before she looked away. Another parent engaged her in a conversation as Kajsa grabbed Noah's hand.

"C'mon, Dad, let's go. I'm starving," Kajsa said.

"Me too," said Adelynn, grabbing his other hand.

Noah resisted, shooting Cassie another glance. "Why don't you change out of your dance shoes first?"

"We can do that in the car. C'mon." Adelynn continued to tug.

"But it's wet outside, and you don't want to ruin your new shoes, right? And besides, I need to ask your teacher something before we go."

"What?" said Kajsa.

"Just a question," he said. "So go take off your shoes and—"

"Miss Cassie!" Adelynn shouted across the room, interrupting the conversation between Cassie and another parent.

Cassie looked her way. "Yes, Adelynn?"

"My dad needs to ask you a question."

The room became quiet, and all eyes came to rest on Noah. Awesome. He shuffled his feet, making a mental note to have a discussion with his daughters about tact.

Cassie said a few last words to the parent she'd been talking to, then headed Noah's way. The slow and careful way she moved wasn't at all like the way she danced. Where was the smile with the dimple that she gave so easily to her students?

Her perfectly shaped eyebrows arched when she neared. "Yes?"

"Uh . . ." His daughters waited impatiently, and a few of the other parents continued to flick glances his way. What now? It wasn't like Noah could blurt out, "Hey, just wondering what your favorite flavor of ice cream is" without sounding strange. But Cassie was looking at him expectantly, so he had to say *something*. "I was just, uh . . . wondering about next fall and whether or not you'll be teaching . . . again." That was stupid. Of course she'd be teaching. It was her career.

"Daddy," Kajsa whined, apparently not happy with the idea of more lessons next fall.

"Not for you," he amended. "For Adi."

"Really?" Adelynn squealed, obviously delighted. Great. Now Noah was committed to more lessons next fall whether he could afford them or not.

Cassie gave him a strange look. "Yes, I'll be teaching. But I don't have a schedule set in stone yet. And the location might change as well. When it gets a little closer, I'll let you know."

Oh good, a location change. Come fall, if money was too tight, Noah could use that as a way out. "Sounds good," he said, trying desperately to think of a way to segue into a conversation about desserts. Had this been Becky's plan all along? Giving him a question that wouldn't be the easiest to

33

work into a casual conversation? Who talked about ice cream in the middle of winter, anyway?

"That it?" Cassie finally said, taking a step back.

"No," blurted Noah. "I mean yes. I mean . . . yes." He cringed. It was time to leave. Now. "Grab your stuff, girls. It's time to go." Noah ushered his girls out the door as fast as he could, cursing Becky's name the entire time.

Five

THE DOOR OPENED with a squeak, revealing Becky's petite body. But when Cassie glanced beyond her friend and spied Noah standing on her front porch, her answering smile froze in place. It was Friday morning, the day Becky—and only Becky—was supposed to help her with her basement plans. What was *he* doing here? Noah Mackie had an unnerving effect on Cassie, and she didn't know why. Just seeing him made her heart jumpy and her hands feel shaky—and not in a good, exciting way. In an anxious, almost fearful way.

From the way Noah's eyes widened at the sight of her, Cassie could tell he was just as surprised to see her as she was to see him. Which meant that Becky was still up to her matchmaking efforts.

"Hey, Cass!" said Becky brightly, as if nothing out of the ordinary was going on. "I hope it's okay that I coerced Noah into coming. He's the general contractor who—"

"No I'm not," he cut in.

Becky rolled her eyes. "Sorry. He's the *almost*-general

contractor who helped Justin and I with our basement. He's brilliant, I'm telling you. And affordable."

Affordable? Oh no. Was Becky expecting Cassie to hire him? Was he expecting to be hired? Suddenly, knowing Becky didn't seem like much of a blessing anymore.

Not knowing what else to do, Cassie opened the door wider to let them in. She reluctantly led the way to her basement and showed them the plans she'd drawn. Becky asked a few questions to orient herself, then announced she loved them. They were perfect.

Cassie smiled, relieved.

Noah, on the other hand, studied the plans with his brows drawn together in thought. He walked over to the one wall that had been erected and tapped it, as if checking to see how sturdy it was. "What's this for?"

Cassie cleared her throat. "My late husband put it up before he passed away. It will need to come down."

Noah slipped through the two-by-fours into the space on the other side of the studs. He pointed at what appeared to be a large circular cap on the ground. "Know what this is?"

"No," said Cassie. She hadn't really noticed it before.

"It's plumbing for where your toilet is supposed to go. And this"—he tapped a black pipe that ran up through the far end of the wall—"is for a sink. And over here—a shower or tub. "

Cassie frowned. A bathroom right there? Why? It was in the middle of the room—the last place she'd want it.

"Oh, that's not good," said Becky.

"Did you build this house?" Noah asked, still watching Cassie.

She shook her head. "No. We—I mean *I*—am the second owner."

"And you don't have the original basement plans?"

"No." At least Cassie didn't think she did. Maybe Landon had filed it away somewhere, but she had no idea where that might be.

Noah let out a breath. "Well, if you want to change locations of the bathroom, it's going to involve ripping out a bunch of this concrete and redoing some plumbing—which isn't going to be cheap. Or easy. Or fun."

Cassie felt like slumping to the ground and crying. She'd spent months on those plans. *Months.* And now, in less than five minutes, Noah Mackie had essentially destroyed them. She was back to square one, stuck with a horrible place for a bathroom. What now? Was this Fate's way of saying that an in-home dance studio wasn't meant to be? It sure felt that way.

Becky gave her a look of sympathy and put her arm around Cassie. "Don't worry. Noah will figure out a better plan. He has never let anyone down."

Noah shot Becky an incredulous what-are-you-talking-about look before he went back to perusing the plans. Once more, he examined the empty space. "So you want a family room, a dance studio, a bathroom, and some space for a waiting area. Is that right?"

"Yes," said Cassie weakly. Though at this point, she'd settle for just the studio.

"I'm sure she'll want a few storage closets as well," inserted Becky.

"Of course she does," Noah said dryly, as though she'd just asked the impossible. He continued to look around Cassie's basement while she continued to fight off tears of frustration. She wouldn't cry. She wouldn't. If there was one thing she'd learned from Landon, it was that you didn't show weakness in front of others. He'd hated weakness.

Silence reigned as Noah walked the length and breadth of her basement. He unclipped a measuring tape from his pocket and stretched it out, writing numbers down as he went.

Stupid drains and pipes, thought Cassie. *Whose idea was it to put the bathroom there anyway?* She wanted to call them up and give them a piece of her mind. *You've ruined everything!*

"Would you be okay with a smaller family room space?" Noah finally asked, pulling Cassie from her self-pitying thoughts.

"What?"

"A smaller living space down here—would you be okay with that?"

"How much smaller?"

"About fifteen-by-fifteen. Just big enough for a little sectional and a fireplace in that nook over there."

Fireplace? Cassie hadn't even considered that. "Can I put a fireplace down here?"

"I assumed that's what this square is for." Noah pointed to a rectangle on her drawing that she'd X'd out.

"That was supposed to be a storage closet, but I like the idea of a fireplace better." Actually, she loved the idea of a fireplace. The basement was always so cold. It would be nice to flip a switch and turn on some heat and charm. Yes, she was now set on having a fireplace in the basement.

"And yeah, I'd be okay with a smaller living space," she finally said. "Why? What are you thinking?"

"Well, if you keep the bathroom where it's at and put a small shower in it instead of a tub, it could act as the divider between your two spaces. You can add a short, Jack-and-Jill-style hallway with doors on either side so you can still access the studio from inside the house. But then the bathroom can be used for both spaces, depending on which door you leave unlocked. The drawback is that your students would have to cross the dance area to get to it."

That was only a small drawback, and definitely one Cassie could live with. Something that felt like hope flared in her chest. Why hadn't she thought of that configuration herself? Because in her mind, the bathroom belonged tucked up against a wall near the entrance to her basement. She'd never thought about putting it in the middle.

"Your dance studio would lose about a foot on this side, but you'd gain two over here. And by moving the bathroom there, it would allow you some space over here for a wider storage closet and a drinking fountain.

"Oh, I'd love a drinking fountain," Cassie blurted. Why hadn't she thought of that either? She figured she'd just get one of those water coolers and keep it stocked with small cups, but an actual fountain would be ideal.

"Isn't that what this circle is right here?" Again, Noah gestured to her plans.

Cassie had to laugh at that. "No, that's supposed to be a coat rack. But that's okay. The girls can leave their stuff on chairs or something. I'd rather have a drinking fountain."

"Oh," said Noah. "Why not just screw a bunch of hooks along this wall for the girls to hang their stuff on?"

"Told you he's good," inserted Becky.

Cassie suddenly felt like crying for an entirely different reason. What had been destroyed moments before was now new and improved. She had to resist the urge to throw her arms around Noah and hug him. He was officially hired.

"Thank you both so much. I should have called you months ago, Becky."

"I didn't do anything. It was all Noah."

It was true. "Thank you, Noah. So, so much. If you want the job, it's yours."

Noah hesitated for a moment. "On one condition."

"Name it."

"Tell me your favorite ice cream flavor."

For some reason, Becky started laughing. Then she made up some excuse about needing a drink and disappeared upstairs.

Cassie arched an eyebrow. "My favorite what?"

"Flavor of ice cream."

"Why?"

"Because." He shrugged, then shuffled his feet. "It,

39

uh . . . tells me a lot about a person. I guess you can say it's my way of sizing someone up."

Cassie was becoming more lost by the second. "How so?"

He kicked at a two-by-four at the base of the unfinished wall. "It's all about the flavor. Someone who likes mint and chip, for example—like Kajsa—is enthusiastic and creative, with a hint of scattered. Adi, on the other hand, prefers cookies and cream, which means she can be both cheeky and sweet."

Huh? That made no sense. "What's your favorite?"

"Only the best one out there—cookie dough."

Her lips began to twitch. She still had no idea where he was going with this, but it was kind of funny. "What does that say about you? That you haven't grown up yet?"

"No," came his reply. "It tells you that I'm complex, interesting, and . . . a little doughy." Cassie snickered at that, and he shoved the tape measure back in his pocket. "Now it's your turn."

"What if I don't have a favorite?"

"Impossible. Everyone has one."

"Well, maybe I don't."

"And maybe you just don't want to tell me."

Cassie chewed on her lower lip, wondering why they were having this conversation. Before Landon, butter pecan had always been her go-to flavor. But Landon had been allergic to pecans and didn't care for ice cream in general, so Cassie hadn't eaten it in years. Was butter pecan still her favorite? She honestly didn't know.

Noah's striking blue eyes watched her. "Don't you like ice cream?"

Cassie squirmed, feeling like she was being put on the spot. "I do—at least, I used to. But maybe I don't anymore."

She frowned. If she liked ice cream that much, wouldn't she have craved it sometime during the past few years? Wouldn't she have filled her freezer with it after Landon

40

died? Maybe it was a situation of out of sight, out of mind, or maybe she really didn't like it. The next time Cassie hit the grocery store, she'd have to give butter pecan another try.

In the meantime . . . "What about my favorite color instead?"

Noah shook his head. "Sorry. It has to be ice cream. And I think I already know your favorite color. Pink, right?"

"Why do you say that?"

He stepped closer and tugged lightly on her pink scarf, making the basement feel hot and small all of a sudden. Her face flushed.

"Every time I see you, you're wearing this color. There's a pink throw on your couch upstairs and pink hand towels in your bathroom. And I'm willing to bet that you're planning to plant pink flowers in the spring."

"Wow, you're observant." Cassie suddenly felt suffocated by the color. She fiddled with the scarf, loosening it from around her neck.

"Am I right?" he said.

"I'm not sure. Can favorite things change?"

"What do you mean?"

"Well," said Cassie. "Pink used to be one of my favorites, but now I might be sick of it. So maybe it's not anymore."

"Ah," said Noah, leaning his shoulder against one of the two-by-fours. "In that case, then yeah, favorites can change. Happens to me all the time."

"Your favorite color changes a lot?" Cassie pictured him spinning a color wheel every morning to decide what to wear for the day. Not that he struck her as the sort of guy who actually cared what he wore.

"No. It's been blue since I was a kid. But my favorite daughter changes all the time."

Cassie's eyes widened. Who had a favorite kid? And what kind of person admitted it out loud? "You're joking, I hope."

"Nope." His eyes glinted at her in a teasing way. "The first one to give me a hug after a long day becomes my favorite. Or the one who's the happiest, the one who faces a fear, or the one who tries something new and fails, but keeps trying anyway." He paused. "Yeah, my favorite daughter changes on an hourly basis. But in the end, it balances out."

"Oh." A strange sensation squeezed at Cassie's heart. It had been a long time since she'd been charmed by a man, and yet that was exactly what Noah had just done. She didn't like it.

Hooking her thumb over her shoulder, Cassie took a step back. "Um . . . do you want a drink or anything?"

He pushed away from the wall. "No thanks. I need to get going. If it works for you, I'll put together a bid this weekend and drop it by on Monday."

"Yeah, that works." She started walking toward the stairs, then stopped and glanced over her shoulder. "Out of curiosity, if you're not a general contractor yet, what exactly are you?"

He thought for a moment. "Most people in my situation would say they're between jobs. But a more accurate description would be to say that I'm Becky's latest project."

Cassie's confusion must have shown on her face because he added, "I got laid off about a month ago, and Becky keeps finding me odd jobs to keep the paychecks coming. Once the weather warms and construction companies get busy again, I'm hoping to find something more permanent. But until then, I'm happy to be of service."

"And I'm happy you're available."

When his lips tightened into a grin, Cassie realized how that comment could have been taken. Her face infused with heat. "For the job, I mean."

"I know." Still grinning, he brushed past her and headed up the stairs, leaving her with the same anxiety she'd felt when she first saw him standing on her doorstep.

What had she gotten herself into?

Six

THE ONE-DIMENSIONAL LINES on the laptop screen connected and intersected to form a two-dimensional plan of
Cassie's basement. As Noah stared at it, the shapes seemed to
rise off the screen, taking on yet another dimension. In his
mind, he could see what the family room would look like
with the fireplace and mantle. He could see the shiny wood
floor of the dance studio, along with rows of recessed
lighting to brighten up the space. He could see the doors
connecting the two spaces, the bathroom, the closets, the
nook for Cassie's stereo system—everything. The finished
product was there, buried beneath all the shapes, lines and
measurements.

Noah loved design. More than that, he loved taking that
design and turning it into something tangible. Something
real. Something that smelled like freshly sanded wood, new
paint, and . . . home. This was what he wanted to do more
than anything. Design. Build. Create. He wanted to be
involved in all of it.

In the construction industry, there were drafters, architects, concrete crews, framers, flooring specialists, HVAC guys, stone masons, finishers, etc. And then there were the general contractors who oversaw it all. Which was why he aspired to become one himself. It was a career that allowed him to be around from start to finish.

But what seemed like an achievable goal only months before now felt impossible. General contractors were a dime a dozen. Competition was fierce, the market slow, and opportunities scarce. But, like his dad used to say, "Where there's a will, there's a way," and Noah definitely had the will. Now all he had to do was find the way.

No sweat.

The clock changed from eleven-fifty-nine to midnight. He stretched his arms over his head, enjoying the slight release it gave his muscles. He should probably get some sleep, but this was his most productive time of day, when the girls were in bed. So he pulled out a calculator and a pad of paper and got to work. He'd break down the costs of the project, put together an estimate, and take everything to Cassie tomorrow.

"Daddy?" a quiet voice sounded behind him. Noah spun around and spotted Adelynn in the doorway. Her beautiful brown eyes were wet with tears as she squinted through the light at him.

Noah opened his arms to her, and she promptly crawled on to his lap and snuggled close. "What's the matter, princess?"

"I had a bad dream."

"Want to tell me about it?"

"A bad man was chasing me. I saw Mommy and ran to her, but when I got close, she ran away." Fresh tears filled her eyes as she looked up. "Why did she do that?"

Noah frowned. His girls didn't usually have bad dreams, and he couldn't remember them ever dreaming about Angie—especially not in a negative way. Where had this

44

come from? He pulled Adelynn close and rubbed her back. "It was just a dream, sweetie. It didn't mean anything."

"But remember when I dreamed about living in a balloon house? You said that meant I was going to have a lot of balloons at my birthday party. And I did."

Noah stifled a groan. Sometimes he really wished his girls' memories were more like his: spotty. But they were both too sharp for their own good, and Noah had to learn to think on his toes—something that was difficult to do after midnight.

He sighed. "You're right. Sometimes dreams can mean something, but sometimes they're just dreams and don't mean anything at all. If I dreamed about a big, purple dinosaur coming to eat dinner, do you think that means we'd really have to make room for a big, purple dinosaur?"

Adelynn shook her head, but uncertainty still clouded her eyes. "Did you dream about a big, purple dinosaur?"

"Well, no, but—"

"Then that doesn't count, Daddy."

Once again, she had him. At times like these, Noah missed Angie more than usual. She would have been able to come up with something plausible. And she never would have bought a bunch of extra balloons for a birthday party in an attempt to make a dream come true. But Angie wasn't here to explain why she'd run away from their daughter in a nightmare.

"Do you miss Mommy?" Noah asked.

Her little eyebrows scrunched together. "Sometimes. I wish she was here to do my hair really cute for school or come on field trips with our class like Beth's mom does. Sometimes, I wish . . ." Her voice trailed off, as though she was worried she'd hurt her dad's feelings.

"What do you wish?" he encouraged.

"That I had a mommy." The words came out as almost a whisper, and she kept her head down, refusing to look at him.

Noah's heart constricted. He thought of all the field trips he'd had to miss. How his hands that were so skilled at cutting wood were worthless when it came to anything hair related. How his dinners weren't nearly as good as Emma's or Becky's or how the girls never knew who'd be picking them up from dance.

Suddenly, the life Noah offered his daughters felt like it wasn't enough anymore. Did Becky and Emma see it too? Was that the reason they were encouraging him to get out and start dating again?

The revelation settled like a heavy brick in his stomach.

He snuggled Adelynn closer. "How about if I sing you a bedtime song?"

"You can't sing, Daddy."

"Gee, thanks," said Noah. "Well then, maybe I can come lay beside you until you fall asleep instead."

Adelynn nodded, and Noah picked her up, throwing her over his shoulder like a sack of potatoes. A giggle sounded, and Noah smiled. At least he was still good for something.

Cassie straightened the salt shaker on the kitchen counter then glared at it, immediately pushing it back. She didn't used to be so OCD, but no matter how hard she tried not to be, she couldn't stop herself. Landon had ingrained in her that everything had a place, and that's where it belonged. But no matter how hard she tried to stop being that way, she constantly found herself organizing and tidying, scouring and vacuuming. It was the only thing to do when she didn't have anything else to do, and doing something was better than doing nothing. Maybe this was who she was now—a person obsessed with appearance.

Was it possible to become someone you didn't want to be?

Cassie's house belonged on the cover of *An Organizer's Guide to Frustration-free Living*, and yet her life felt so disorganized. So frustrating. Maybe that's why she continued to put everything in its place even though Landon was no longer around to get after her if she didn't. Otherwise, she'd be even more lost.

A loud knock interrupted her thoughts and made her jump, tipping the salt shaker over. She quickly set it upright, pushed it back in its place, and swept the granules off the counter and into her palm. She tossed the salt into the trashcan as she made her way to the front of her house. Another knock vibrated the door right before she pulled it open to find Noah Mackie on her doorstep.

"Hey" was all he said.

Her heart gave an involuntary little skip, and Cassie resisted the urge to run and hide. He was too handsome, too talented, too charming, and too available. He scared her the way Landon never had, but should have.

Her fingers continued to grip the knob as she stood on the threshold, unable to do something as simple as invite him inside. She nodded toward the papers he held in his hand. "Is that the estimate?"

"It is. Though I realized last night that you never gave me a budget to work with. So I added in everything I thought you might want, gave you a large allowance for things like flooring, bathroom amenities, and the fireplace, then built in a cushion for some extras. So if it seems really high, that's why. We can always scale things back and go with less expensive flooring. That's up to you." He held the pages out to her. "Would you like me to go through it with you?"

"No, that's okay." Cassie took the plans from him, making sure to avoid touching him in the process. "I'll look it all over and call you if I have any questions."

"Okay," he agreed. "I just finished up another project,

so I can get started on your basement whenever you're ready. Just let me know."

"I will."

He nodded and turned to go.

"Oh, and Noah?"

He stopped and twisted back to face her, one eyebrow quirked in silent question.

"Thank you."

"No problem."

Cassie watched him walk away, unable to pull her eyes away from his relaxed, yet confident stride. He had a laid-back manner about him that made it seem like nothing ever got to him, and yet Cassie didn't trust it. People weren't always what they seemed. She'd learned that one the hard way.

Seven

NOAH KNELT ON the cold concrete and plugged his phone into an old set of speakers. He set it to an upbeat playlist that included songs by Foo Fighters, Evanescence, Aerosmith, and Green Day—some of his favorite bands. Then he cranked up the volume and began drilling the holes through the studs for all the wiring. The HVAC had been run, the walls roughed in, and now it was time for the electrical. If he could get it done by the end of the week, he'd be ahead of schedule and could probably get the walls drywalled and prepped for paint before the week of spring break. Hopefully Cassie wouldn't mind if he took that week off to spend with his girls.

All in all, things were looking up. His old boss had even called the week prior, saying that work was picking up and they'd probably have a job for him by the end of April. The timing couldn't have been better. He'd take time off the week of spring break, finish up Cassie's basement, and pick up where he'd left off with his old job.

As he fished the cable through the newly drilled hole, a

muffled, musical sound invaded, not quite drowning out the Pearl Jam song he was listening to, but definitely ruining it. Noah walked over to his speakers and turned the volume down. The sound of fiddles, flutes, and—was that an accordion?—filtered down through the ceiling. It was that strange Irish music. Loud banging soon followed, making it sound as though Cassie was tap dancing across the floor above him.

He glanced up and frowned. Why wasn't she wearing those ballet-type shoes like his girls wore? The ones with soft soles that produced quiet steps.

At first, Noah tried not to listen, then he tried not to care. Cassie couldn't keep at it forever. But when the accordion, fiddles, and banging dragged on for an hour or more, Noah couldn't take it any longer. So he cranked up his music, turning it loud enough to drown out a sound that should never be referred to as music. Torture, maybe. Music, no way.

The banging on the ceiling stopped, and Noah resumed working, grateful that Cassie seemed to be done. But then the crazy, Irish noise increased in volume to the point that it overrode Linkin Park, which, Noah had to admit, was a feat. It wasn't an easy band to crowd out, though the duet of the two genres was not a sound anyone should ever have to hear.

He winced as he trotted over to his speakers and turned up the volume again, this time to the max. The Irish noise followed suit, growing louder and louder until it completely drowned out whatever song Noah's pitiful little speakers played. He stared at the ceiling, wondering what sort of sound system the woman had upstairs. It was nothing less than awesome.

Noah brushed the sawdust from his hands, powered off the speakers, and jogged up the stairs. At the top, he knocked, but there was no way she would be able to hear anything with that racket going on. So he cracked the door and poked his head through. No one was in sight.

It was difficult to tell where the music was coming from; the speakers seemed to be everywhere. But Noah had already seen the left side of her house, where there was no room to dance, so he turned right and walked cautiously down the sleek, dark hardwood floor. He paused when Cassie came in sight, her legs and feet moving so quickly in skipping/kicking motions that it made them hard to follow.

The grating music faded to the background as Cassie popped in and out of his line of sight. She had an almost regal bearing with perfect posture and long legs that drew Noah's attention. Not only was her body beautifully formed, but the way she moved through the fast, intricate steps captivated him. She wore what appeared to be clogging shoes, which would explain the loud banging. Only now it didn't sound like banging. It sounded like a cool drum accompaniment to the music.

When her legs carried her out of sight once again, Noah took a few steps forward and leaned against the wall, folding his arms. He continued to watch until her feet led her in a circular motion and she caught him staring.

Her eyes widened, and she immediately stopped dancing. She quickly spun around and shut off the music. Her chest and shoulders rose and fell from the exertion of heavy exercise.

Wow, she had nice lines.

"I'm sorry," he said. "I tried to knock, but you didn't hear. I just wanted to see what sort of stereo system could completely drown out my music downstairs."

She glanced over her shoulder at him, looking almost skeptical. "You're not upset?"

"Upset? No. In awe? Yes. I want your speakers. What brand are they?"

Her eyebrows scrunched together in a flummoxed expression. "I don't know for sure. They belonged to my late husband. All I know is he loved music, wanted the best of the best, and had speakers wired into nearly every room. I'm sorry about drowning out your music. I just really need to finish the choreography of a dance before my class tomorrow, and I couldn't keep the beat straight with your music in the background. I also can't figure out how to keep the sound to just this room. There are too many buttons, and I'm afraid I'll mess something up if I touch anything."

"Well, you obviously know how to work the volume," teased Noah, walking toward her.

Her face flushed, and the color clashed with her hair. It was kind of adorable to see this vulnerable side to her. Maybe she wasn't quite as refined or perfect as she first appeared.

"Let's see here." Noah powered on the receiver then scanned the knobs and buttons until he found one called Input. As he slowly turned the knob, the music quieted, sounding like it was coming from the next room over.

"How did you do that?" Cassie leaned closer, and the smell of sweat mixed with sawdust mingled in the air.

"I'm magic."

"Will you teach me? Please?"

Noah smiled. "This is a multi-room receiver. All you have to do is turn this knob, and the music will switch from one room to the next. Turn it back upright, and you'll get music everywhere."

Cassie gave it a try, and a tentative smile played across her lips as the sounds changed. Noah liked being the one who'd put it there.

"How, exactly, do you get your feet to move that fast?" he asked.

Her smile widened, revealing that elusive dimple. "Lots and lots and lots of practice."

"Have you ever thought of dancing to, you know, more modern music?"

"Are you calling Irish jigs outdated?"

"I wouldn't dare for fear you'd trample all over me with those shoes."

She laughed softly. It had a lilting ring to it that Noah

found intriguing. "For the competitions, the girls are only allowed to dance to Irish music. If Adi or Kajsa continue to take lessons next year, they'll be able to compete and then you'll understand."

Noah nodded. "I just think you could totally rock it to Pearl Jam."

The smile disappeared from her face. "I don't like hard rock."

"What about plain old pop rock then?"

Her shoulders moved up and down in a semi-shrug. "I'll think about it."

"You should. I know my girls would love that, and if you chose a Taylor Swift song, Kajsa might even enjoy it."

"Yeah, maybe."

"In the meantime," said Noah, "maybe we should talk about putting in some good sound-proofing insulation in the ceiling and walls of your studio."

"And the sooner the better, right?" she said dryly.

He chuckled. "I'm only thinking of you."

"Right."

"Seriously. Some day you might have a napping baby or kids trying to do homework or—"

"No. I won't." Her body stiffened as she turned back to her stereo. "Do whatever you think is best. I really need to get back to choreographing."

Noah wasn't sure what he'd said to ruin the camaraderie they had going, but he wished he could take it back. Cassie was fun to talk to when she let her guard down a little. She was also interesting in a slightly mysterious way, and it would be nice to get to know her a little better. Why didn't she like hard rock? Why didn't she have a favorite ice cream flavor? And why were there fluffy, pink towels hanging in her modernized half bath and from the handle of her sleek, stainless steel oven door?

There was a story behind it all, Noah could feel it.

Cassie reminded him of a brain teaser game his father

had once given him. It consisted of two metal tubes that spiraled around in the shape of a cursive "e" and were connected at the center. Noah's job? To un-connect them. But the metal had been too thick to fit through each other, so Noah had immediately given it back to his father, saying it was impossible. His father turned his back to Noah, fiddled with the toy for a few seconds, and turned around, holding a metal *e* in each of his hands. A few wiggles of his wrists later, they were reconnected, and his dad handed it back.

"Nothing's impossible," he'd said.

After that, Noah had spent hours fiddling with the stupid toy, only to toss it down in frustration at the end of the day. "How did you do it, Dad?" he'd demanded that night.

"Keep at it. You'll figure it out eventually."

And Noah had. Eventually. At first, it had happened by accident. He'd been playing with the toy, and suddenly, as if by magic, the two pieces fell apart from each other. Then, as his father had promised, over time, he'd finally learned that if he twisted the metal in a certain way, he could easily separate them the way his father had.

Maybe that was what Cassie was like. To Noah, she was two separate things: a pink hand towel and sleek, contemporary fixtures. But if he got to know her better, maybe he'd find a way to put them together and figure her out.

The question was: did he care enough to try?

Maybe. Maybe not.

With slow and thoughtful steps, Noah returned to the basement and finished fishing the cable through the walls. Only after he was done did he realize that the Irish music never came on again.

Eight

"GIRLS! WHAT'S TAKING so long? You're going to be late for school, and I'm going to be late for work," Noah called.

"I can't find my boots." Kajsa's voice echoed down the hall.

"My hair is ugly," complained Adelynn. "I told you I shouldn't go to bed with it wet, Daddy."

Noah entered the girls' room to find Kajsa's bare feet sticking out from under the bed and Adelynn trying to pull a brush from her tangled hair.

"Are your boots under there?" he asked Kajsa as he grabbed the brush from Adelynn's hands and started working it through her long, blond hair. Every stroke made her grimace.

"I found one," came Kajsa's muffled reply. "Oh, there's the other one." She wiggled out from under the bed, wearing a grin and a hairstyle that could be used for an object lesson on disorder and chaos. Noah awkwardly tried to wrap an elastic around Adelynn's hair so he could work on Kajsa's.

"Dad, that ponytail is lopsided and too loose." Adelynn frowned at her reflection.

Behind her, Kajsa rolled her eyes as she yanked on her favorite cowboy boots. "Ready," she announced.

"I think we need to brush your hair first," said Noah as he attempted to tighten and center Adelynn's ponytail.

"Can't I just run over to Aunt Emma's really quick?" begged Adelynn. "She never takes long."

"You know we can't do that anymore, Adi. She gets really sick in the morning and needs her rest." Noah gave Adelynn's head a pat, signaling he was done. Then he tried to get Kajsa to stand still so he could brush her hair.

"Dad, it's fine," Kajsa whined, dodging his attempts.

Adelynn continued to glare at her reflection. "I am so not going to school looking like this."

Noah was about to give up on Kajsa and force Adi to get in the car when he spied a vacuum in the corner. It sparked an idea, and he handed the brush back to Kajsa. "Here. You untangle it. But do it quick."

Then he grabbed the vacuum, turned it on, and lugged it over to where Adelynn stood with her glare now trained on him.

"I thought you said we had to go," she said, raising her voice above the whine of the vacuum.

"Hold still." Noah pulled the elastic from her hair, wrapped it tightly around the handheld adaptor of the vacuum, and began sucking all of her hair into it.

"Daddy!" Adelynn's dark eyes grew wide with horror. "What are you doing?"

Noah quickly slid the elastic from the adaptor to Adelynn's hair, creating a tight ponytail that was perfectly centered at the back of her head. He smiled in satisfaction. "There. You're done. Kajsa, get over here."

"That was weird, Dad," said Adelynn, but at least she no longer complained about a lopsided ponytail. Kajsa came willingly, which was a first. Apparently, she wanted to experience what it felt like to have her hair sucked into a vacuum too.

In no time at all, Noah had his girls ready to go. He handed them lunches with sloppy PB&J sandwiches inside, shuffled them out the door, and watched them climb on the bus and wave goodbye.

A chime sounded, and Noah pulled his phone from his pocket, finding a text from Cassie.

I won't be home this morning to let you in, so I left the basement door unlocked. Feel free to turn that noise you call music up as loud as you want.

Noah smiled. *If my music is noise, yours is pain. Unless you're dancing to it, that is. Then I don't mind it.*

Lucky for you I'm sending the girls home with a CD of Irish music next week to practice with. The darling way they dance will have you loving it in no time.

Noah imagined the sound of bagpipes blaring through his house with Adelynn skipping up and down the hallway and Kajsa yelling at her to stop. Somehow, he didn't think he'd come to love it anytime soon.

Will there be a Taylor Swift song on that CD? he wrote back, hoping she'd given his suggestion a little more thought.

Not this time, came her response.

Your favorite ice cream must be the boring flavor of vanilla, Noah wrote back. Then he paused with his thumb over the Send button, wondering if the teasing comment would offend her. Or maybe it would make her laugh. She obviously had a sense of humor, but every once in awhile Noah would say something she didn't find funny at all.

He hit Send anyway and waited, almost holding his breath. A minute passed before his phone chimed again.

I'm beginning to understand why yours is cookie dough and not peaches and cream. Maybe there really is something to your ice cream psychology.

Noah laughed. Yes, she definitely had a sense of humor.

"What's so funny?" Becky's voice sounded from across the street.

Noah shoved his phone in his back pocket and raised his voice so she could hear him. "Cassie." When Becky's mouth lifted into a knowing smile, Noah pointed a finger in her direction. "Don't start."

The knowing smile remained. "Figure out what her favorite ice cream flavor is yet?"

"She doesn't have one."

She shook her head, rejecting his answer. "Everyone has a favorite. You just have to work a little harder to figure hers out. You promised, remember?"

"And you tricked me. Somehow, you knew the answer wouldn't come easy, didn't you?"

"Maybe." She chuckled and waved. "Don't let me keep you. Enjoy your day."

"Yeah, you too." Noah hopped in his truck and drove away, allowing his thoughts to veer in Cassie's direction. How did she get her ponytails to always look so neat and centered? Was that another thing that took a lot of practice, or was it one of those talents that some people had and some people didn't, like Emma's way with a paintbrush?

Noah shook his head and redirected his thoughts to where they should be: Cassie's basement. Spring break was only a week and a half away. But if Kevin or Justin would be available to help him hang drywall this weekend, by the end of next week he should have everything ready to be primed and painted.

And then he'd take a week off to spend with his princesses.

Cassie pulled her damp hair into a sloppy bun on the top of her head and slipped into some pink yoga pants and a pink tank top. Landon had hated the color on her because it clashed with her hair. Not long after they were married, she'd found the few pink tops she owned and her favorite pink sweats shoved into a trash bag by the garage door.

"You know I hate that color," he'd said when she asked him about it. "I don't understand why I had to be the one to get rid of all that stuff. If you respected me at all, you wouldn't have brought it into my house."

His house. That's the way he had always looked at things even though they'd bought the home together. But Landon had been the one to pick out the flooring, the fixtures, and the furniture for the remodel. So in that respect, it really had been his house. Still was, in fact. Cassie would change it all if she could, but the bulk of the life insurance money was going toward the basement renovation, so the rest would have to wait.

After Landon's funeral, Cassie had driven straight to Target. She'd filled her cart with pink towels, pink shirts, pink flannel pajama bottoms, fuzzy pink slippers, and whatever else she could find in that color—even sticky notes. It was because of Landon that she wore something pink almost every day even though she was really coming to detest the color. It reminded her that she was her own person who didn't have to answer to anyone.

She padded down the hardwood hallway into the sleek, modern kitchen. There was a time when she thought Landon had done well with his choices. The dark, simple lines of the wood initially looked beautiful to her, complimenting the stainless steel appliances and granite counters. But over the two years she'd spent with him, Cassie had come to hate it all. She couldn't put her feet up on the coffee table for fear of scuffing it, couldn't curl up in the uncomfortable armchair, and too much time had been wasted wiping down the stainless steel appliances and dusting all the dark wood. What she'd thought would be a beautiful and comfortable home became a cool and distant dwelling.

Cassie sighed when she saw the dishes in the sink. She'd overslept that morning and had rushed out the door without wiping the toast crumbs from the counter or rinsing out the pan and bowl she'd used. Now they were sitting in her water-spotted sink, coated in dried oatmeal.

It had been a long day. Two of her classes had gotten a little out of control, and she had no desire to scrub the dishes clean right now. Or mop the floor, for that matter. But it needed to be done. So she inhaled a deep breath and turned up the volume on a favorite Beatles' song. As she scrubbed her dishes, her humming became singing, and her body began to move with the beat of the music. As she pulled the mop from the closet, Faith Hill's "Me" came on, and Cassie cranked up the volume more.

It wasn't a song most people knew—just a little two-letter title listed as number nine on the *Faith* album. But the moment Cassie had first heard it, she'd fallen in love with it. Don't change who you are to impress someone else—that was the message—and one Cassie's youthful, daydreamish heart had clung to. She'd wanted to marry a man who wouldn't want to change her, who'd cherish and love her for her. And she thought she had. When they were dating, Landon had found her quirks adorable, or, at least he said he did. But the moment they'd uttered their I dos, everything began to change. That song became a mockery of her marriage. So she'd buried the CD at the bottom of a large box containing things from her previous life.

After his car accident, Cassie had stumbled across that old box. She'd pulled out all of her old dance medals, the tattered, stuffed teddy bear that her father had won for her at the county fair, the birthday cards her siblings had made for her over the years, and the three photo albums she'd once made—all filled with evidence of happier times. As she flipped through the pages, it felt like she was looking at someone else—a happy, bubbly, and carefree Cassie who loved to photo bomb her siblings' pictures, play mud football, organize group dates, invent new recipes, and dye her hair pink for Halloween.

Where had that girl gone?

As Cassie set aside that last album, she'd looked down to find that old *Faith* CD. She picked it up, turned it over, and stared at the word "Me" until her vision had blurred. Then she ripped the entire album to her computer, transferred it to her mp3 player, and went straight to that song. As the words sounded, she'd closed her eyes and allowed them entrance into her mind. They weaved around her pain, bringing with them a powerful sensation—one of healing, truth, and determination to never let anyone take the "me" from her again.

The problem was that Cassie wasn't sure who she was anymore. It was like Landon had extracted that fun-loving girl and hidden it somewhere she couldn't find it. All that was left was a wannabe shell.

Cassie didn't even know what her favorite flavor of ice cream was anymore.

The chorus came on, and Cassie forgot all about the floor. She belted out the words, using the mop handle as a microphone. She spun around, executing a few quick-step dance moves and sang her aching heart out.

When a man appeared in her peripheral vision, Cassie simultaneously squealed and jumped. For a moment, she saw Landon in his features, as though he'd come back from the dead to haunt her. But then her vision refocused, and Landon became Noah, leaning against the wall adjacent to the basement stairs with his arms folded and his lips pulled into a small smile.

Wow, he was handsome.

"Noah!" she chided, shoving the mop behind her. "You scared me to death. What are you still doing here?" He never worked past three.

Noah pushed away from the wall and walked toward her, stopping next to the island. "Sorry, I didn't mean to scare you. I forgot to get a measurement that I needed before I hit the store tomorrow. So when my sister invited my girls over for some dessert, I figured I'd run over here and take care of it. You didn't answer when I rang, and the basement door was still open, so I let myself in. I hope that's okay."

"Yes, that's fine. I haven't had a chance to lock up yet." That still didn't explain what he was doing up here, watching her sing and dance. Underneath that nice, handsome exterior, was he really a creep?

Her thought must have been written on her face, because he held up his hand. "Now before you go thinking I'm a peeping Tom or something, I'm only up here because I need to get your okay on something. I heard the music and knocked on your basement door, but you didn't hear me. Then I called out your name—very loudly, I might add—and could have sworn you said, 'Come in.' So I did."

"I never said that." Cassie hadn't heard a thing.

"I figured as much when I saw you dancing with the mop." He smiled. "I had no idea you could sing too."

"I can't." Her cheeks became warm. She quickly shoved the mop in the closet as though it incriminated her in some way.

"I beg to differ." Noah wandered around the island, and, without asking, started scrolling through her playlist.

She rushed forward and tried to grab it from him, but he turned to the side, blocking her with his massive shoulder. "Faith Hill, Imagine Dragons, Chicago, Jordin Sparks—so you *do* like something besides bagpipes."

"There are no bagpipes in Irish music. Now give me that." She tried to shove past him, but his arm was a hard, brick wall.

"Rascal Flatts, Garth Brooks, Coldplay, The Beatles, and . . ." He turned around, his eyebrow raised in question. "St. Elmo's Fire?"

She lunged forward again, but he held her player too high for her to reach. Why did he have to be so tall? "It's a good song," she defended.

"I agree." He pushed play, and the opening beats of "St. Elmo's Fire" filled the room, followed by the rapid drumbeats as the tempo sped up. Still holding the player above his head, Noah started to move to the beat. First, it was his shoulders and head, then his body joined in with hilarious and exaggerated movements. When the lyrics came, he joined in, apparently not caring that he had an audience or a really off-key baritone.

He knew this song, knew the words. And even more surprising was the fact that he seemed to like it as much as she did. But did he feel the words the way she did? Had he ever felt like a prisoner trying to break free? Or was this just a fun, upbeat song to him?

Before Cassie could give it any more thought, he set down her MP3 player and grabbed her hands, gently spinning her around. His fingers had a rough, sandpaper feel to them, but they also felt warm and large and masculine.

"What are you doing?"

"Singing and dancing, duh. Something I really hate to do alone."

"And it's something I *only* do alone."

"Don't give me that. You're a dance teacher."

"Kids are diff—"

"Shh," he said. "It's getting to the good part."

This time, Cassie let him spin her, for no other reason than she didn't know what else to do. It was a foreign thing for her. Landon had never wanted to dance or sing to music. He thought it best to leave it to the professionals and didn't like it when her voice joined in with an artist's. But now here was Noah, belting the words out and trying to coerce her to do the same.

Almost tentatively, she did, purposefully letting her voice get swallowed up with his.

He spun her around so her back was facing him, then pulled her close and whispered in her ear. "C'mon, you can sing louder than that. I heard you. I dare you to out-sing me."

He'd dared her—something one of her brothers would have done and something the old Cassie would have met head on.

The old Cassie. Wasn't that who she was trying to find?

She raised her voice and belted out the words, trying to show him what on-key sounded like.

"That's more like it." He grinned, spinning her around once more—her with bare feet and him with sneakers. The touch of his hand and warmth of his body ignited feelings in her that she had tried so hard to keep buried. But with every conversation, every look, every touch, he'd loosened those feelings more and more, and in that moment, she didn't care. Cassie was lost to the moment.

When "St. Elmo's Fire" came to an end, Noah kept her dancing while REO Speedwagon's "Take it on the Run" began. Cassie was having too much fun to call it quits. The tempo of this song was slower, so Noah dialed it down a notch, pulling her in for a simplified two-step while they continued to try to out-sing each other.

"And even if it is, keep kissin' my hide," Cassie's voice rang out loud.

Noah pulled her to a stop. "What did you just say?"

"Keep kissin' my hide," she repeated, all shyness gone.

He dropped his head back and laughed, a deep guttural sound that shook his entire body, shaking Cassie in the process.

"What's so funny?"

When he looked at her again and there were tears in his eyes. He wiped them away, still laughing. "It's *keep this in mind*—not keep kissin' my hide."

"No, it's not." Cassie pulled away from him and grabbed her MP3 player, starting the song over again. Noah leaned against the counter next to her with that silly grin still fixed on his face. But at least he wasn't laughing anymore.

When the song reached those lyrics again, Cassie listened closely. Sure enough, "Keep this in mind" worked also—and made a lot more sense.

"Told you." Noah chuckled again, then took the mp3 player and set it on the counter, turning the volume down. "But for what it's worth, I like your lyrics a lot better."

"Only because it gave you a reason to laugh," she muttered, feeling like a complete moron. How could she have gotten those lyrics wrong? The right words were so obvious.

"What does 'kissing my hide' mean anyway?"

She shrugged. "I don't know. A less crass way of saying 'kiss my butt'?" That started his laughter all over again, and once again, he had to dry his eyes with the back of his hand.

"I had no idea you could be this funny—or fun," he finally said. "I like this side of you."

And she did too, Cassie realized. But the reminder of what she'd become sucked all the fun from the room. She stared at the dusty floor, wanting to go back to singing and dancing and not remembering that she wasn't the old Cassie anymore. She wasn't the new Cassie either. She was a teenaged equivalent, trying to find herself or whatever that meant.

She turned off the music and cleared her throat. "What exactly do you need my okay on?"

He nudged her arm with his elbow, and when she didn't look at him, his fingers gently guided her chin toward him. His eyes held a tenderness she didn't expect to see.

"I promise I wasn't making fun of you," he said. "You have a beautiful voice, you know how to dance, and you have a fun sense of humor. That's kind of intimidating to a guy like me, so when you sang the lyrics wrong, I couldn't help but tease you about it. I'm sorry if I embarrassed you."

He was so close. She could feel the warmth of his breath and smell the scent of freshly cut lumber. Why did she have to like him so much? "How is teasing different than making fun of someone?"

"There's a world of difference," he said. "Making fun is what you do to people you don't like. Teasing is what you do to people you like and want to get to know better."

Her heart leapt and skipped, dancing an Irish jig on its own. She tried to stamp it down, annoyed that he could stir up these feelings so easily in her.

He released her chin and shoved his hands in his pockets. "As for the reason I came upstairs, I wanted to know how you'd feel about a few minor additions before we start hanging drywall." He fished a folded paper from his back pocket and opened it, smoothing out the creases on the counter. It was a small version of her plans with some hand drawn additions. "I was thinking that instead of a really wide fireplace, you might want to add a built in bookcase for storage. And what would you think about moving the sound system from this corner to here?"

Cassie's arm rubbed against his as she hunched over the plans, feeling all warm and tingly. It took extra effort for her to concentrate on his suggestions, but when she did, she found she really liked them.

"Oh, and one last thing," said Noah. He pulled his phone from his pocket and tapped the screen a few times before holding it out to her. "I dropped by a secondhand shop this morning on my way here and found a vanity I thought you might like for the bathroom. What do you think?"

Only that his close proximity made it so she *couldn't*

think. Cassie took his phone and sidestepped away from his touch. She peered at the darkened photo. The vanity had sleek, contemporary lines and looked almost identical to the other vanities in her house. The ones Landon had picked out.

"It's got some scratches and a broken drawer, but those are easily fixed," he said. "And it'll save you a few hundred bucks."

He'd gone to so much trouble, but there was no way she'd put that vanity in her basement. The cost savings didn't matter. She just couldn't.

"You don't like it." Apparently, Cassie wasn't great at masking her thoughts.

She handed the phone back to him. "I really appreciate that you went to the effort to find it, but it's too contemporary."

"Your entire house is contemporary."

"And it's something I would change if I could afford it."

Noah leaned his hip against the counter and folded his arms, studying her with a perplexed look. "Okay," he said slowly. "If not contemporary, what style do you like?"

She pondered the question for a moment and finally shrugged. "I like antiques." Or, at least she thought she did. Growing up, her mother had a lot of antique pieces throughout the house, and going home always felt so cozy and warm.

"Antiques? Really? That kind of surprises me."

"Why?"

"Because contemporary seems to fit you." He paused. "Although, you do like Irish music, so . . ." He let the sentence hang, and a smile crept across his face.

Cassie didn't return it. How had she gotten to the point where a cold and distant house seemed to fit her? Was that the sort of person Landon had turned her into? The sort of person she'd allowed herself to become?

"I did it again, didn't I?" said Noah. "I said something wrong."

Her eyes flew to his, and she was quick to shake her head. "No. It's just . . . nothing. Never mind."

His fingers touched her arm, sending a jolt through her body. She yanked away, and Noah's hands dropped to his side. "Sorry," he said. "I didn't mean to make you uncomfortable."

Cassie realized how ridiculous she was acting and tried to pull herself together. When her eyes met his again, she sighed. "I'm the one who should be sorry. I'm not sure what's wrong with me. Sometimes I just feel like . . ."

Noah waited, his expression interested.

Cassie was surprised by her desire to confide in him. She never confided in anyone, at least not since Landon happened. But it was like her pent-up feelings had been confined too long, like an expired can of food, and she couldn't hold them in any longer.

"I feel like I don't know who I am anymore," she blurted.

Instead of looking shocked, he nodded. "I understand. I went through that too, after Angie died. It was like part of me died with her, and I haven't felt whole since."

Cassie's gaze shifted to the hardwood floor. He thought he understood but really he had no idea. Maybe no one did. "You had a good marriage then?" she asked quietly.

"It definitely wasn't perfect, and it was far from traditional, but Ang and I were really close. She was my best friend, and losing her was the hardest thing I've ever gone through."

Cassie nodded. What would it be like to be best friends with your spouse? To feel like a part of you went missing when they passed? To truly mourn? She had no idea.

"And yours?" Noah asked tentatively, as though afraid he was overstepping.

She shrugged. "What Landon and I had was more of a puppet/puppeteer relationship. He liked to pull the strings and watch me follow." The moment the words were out,

Cassie wished them back. Yes, Landon should have treated her differently. But he'd only been part of the problem. She should have been strong enough to stand up to him. To walk away.

"Oh," said Noah.

Silence followed, bringing with it an awkward tension that grew and thickened until Noah's voice cut through it. "I take it he was the one who liked contemporary?"

"Yes."

More silence.

"And what was *his* favorite ice cream flavor?"

The question was so unexpected that it actually lifted the corners of Cassie's mouth. "Landon hated ice cream."

"Ah. That explains a lot." Noah said it so matter-of-factly, as though it really did explain something.

"How so?"

"If someone can't find one flavor they like out of the hundreds and thousands out there, then maybe nothing can please them—no matter how smart, beautiful, or great that something is."

Cassie's eyes snapped to his. The warmth and compassion she saw there caused something cold and distant in her heart to become warm and close. She didn't know how to respond, only that she felt like throwing her arms around him and hugging him tight. Tears dampened the corners of her eyes, and she blinked frantically, trying to keep them at bay.

Noah slowly reached a hand out, as though afraid of making her jump again. When she didn't flinch, he tucked a stray lock of hair behind her ear. "Now I just need to figure out what your favorite flavor is."

"What if I don't like ice cream either?" It suddenly felt like something to be very afraid of.

His expression softened. "I guarantee you have a favorite flavor. You just haven't tried it yet."

The room seemed to sway, and Cassie's weight moved

forward, pushing her toward Noah. She fought the desire to fall into him.

Noah smiled and took a step back, putting distance between them. "I should go. I'm sure the girls have downed their dessert by now. So . . . see you tomorrow?"

She nodded and watched him go, feeling like she'd just opened a door that should have been kept locked. Bolted, in fact. Like one of those doors from a fantasy movie with hundreds of locks up and down it. What was she doing? What had she done? She was walking into the exact same trap she'd walked into with Landon.

So much for thinking she was too smart to make the same mistake twice.

Nine

SAM'S ALWAYS PERKY, nearly always cheeky voice blared through the phone in his ear. "Guess who's home?" she said in a sing-song voice, as though the news belonged on the home page of Today.com.

Noah smiled. He loved it when Sam came home for the weekend. She radiated vivaciousness, and everyone adored her. Especially his daughters. "About time. I was beginning to forget what you looked like."

"Impossible," she said. "Kajsa and Adi have my picture on the mirror in their room, and I know for a fact that they'd never let you forget me."

"You got me there."

"Speaking of my two favorite girls, are they available to hang with me tonight? I hear Emma gets them tomorrow while you hang drywall with Kevin, so I should get them tonight. I'll bring pizza, a horse movie, and lots of nail polish."

She was always so good to accommodate both of his

girls. The horse movie was for Kajsa, and the nail polish for Adi. The pizza was loved by all, especially Sam.

"And what am I supposed to do while you three party it up in *my* house?"

"I don't know, you could like . . . take a special someone out to ice cream? Or something?" Her pathetic attempt at innocence made Noah almost laugh.

"Not you, too, Sam." But really, he wasn't surprised that Sam knew about Cassie, or that she was giving him a hard time. The apple only fell inches from the tree in that family.

"Oh wait, what did you say, Mom?" Sam's voice became muffled, like she was covering the phone. And then she was back. "I've just been informed that the certain special someone isn't your type. Why is that, by the way? Do you prefer un-special people?"

"You can tell your mother she's a gossip and is raising a daughter with the same lack of respect for other people's privacy."

"What? I can't tell her that. Our gossip exchanges are the foundation of our amazing mother/daughter bond. You don't want to mess that up, do you? Besides, it's not like you'd ever tell me that you're dating your daughters' dance teacher."

"I'm not dating her."

"Yet," Sam was quick to say. "Which brings us full circle, back to the reason I called to begin with. So, are you going to ask this person who is supposedly not-your-type-but-really-is out for ice cream, or did I come home for nothing?"

"Please don't tell me you drove all the way from Denver just to—"

"Don't flatter yourself," she interrupted. "I came to see the girls. You know I can't stay away from them for long. The fact that I also happen to be offering you a night out is a perk."

Noah chose to ignore the last part, hoping the subject of

his dating life, or lack thereof, would go away. "They'll be thrilled you're in town."

"But *while* I'm here, you might as well do something fun. You know, something that involves . . . I don't know, ice cream, maybe?"

Persistence should have been Sam's middle name. First name, actually. Persistence Meddlesome Kinsey. Yes, that would've fit so much better.

"Speaking of dating," said Noah. "When you came home last month, the girls mentioned something about a really hot guy you met? Someone named Marcus who could kiss like Casanova?"

"I did not tell them that," Sam hissed into the phone. "Well, at least not the Casanova part." Becky's voice intruded as a background noise, followed by Sam's, "It's nothing, Mom. He's just messing with me. You know him."

Noah grinned. "I take it that amazing mother/daughter bond doesn't extend to stories about Marcus, aka Casanova? Because I'd be more than happy to bring Becky up to speed about your um, *interesting* dating life."

"As far as you're concerned, it's nonexistent."

"And as far as you're concerned, mine is too. There are no special or un-special people in my life. Got it?"

Sam huffed. "You're no fun."

The front door burst open, and two tween-aged girls rushed inside, dumping their backpacks on the couch. "Well, it's a good thing *you're* fun because otherwise Adi and Kajsa wouldn't care at all that"—he raised his voice above his daughters' chatter—"*Sam's in town.*"

"Sam's here?" Adelynn shrieked. Both she and Kajsa rushed to the front window to make sure that Sam's car was indeed parked in the driveway across the street. Silly grins appeared on their faces when they saw the yellow bug.

"Can we have a movie night?"

"Can it be a horse movie?"

"Can we paint our nails and do makeovers?"

73

"Can we eat popcorn in the family room?"

The questions came like an electric jackhammer, blasted at Noah over and over and over again.

Sam's laughter rang through the phone. "You can tell them all of the above and more. I'll see them soon."

"Thanks, Sam. You just made their night."

"Just like they'll make mine. Can't wait."

As soon as the call ended, Noah told his daughters to grab a snack and get their homework done. Then he ducked into his room with his phone. Even though he'd downplayed his interest in Cassie, Noah wasn't about to let this opportunity pass.

The call went through to her voicemail, so Noah ended the call and tried sending a text message instead.

Got any plans for tonight? I was thinking about ice cream.

For a moment, Noah hesitated. Was asking her out a good idea? Other than a text message telling him that she'd left the basement door open, Cassie had been MIA the past couple of days. Maybe that was her way of telling him to back off. Or maybe she'd been busy.

Sometimes, it would be really nice to have the ability to read minds.

Noah clicked Send before he could talk himself out if it. Then he waited. And waited some more. After about five minutes, he gave up and returned to his girls to ask them about their days. By the time Sam showed up with the promised pizza, fingernail polish, movie, and popcorn in hand, Cassie still hadn't replied. So Noah gave Sam a welcome home hug, told her thanks a million, and walked outside.

The air was chilly, and he'd forgotten his jacket. So he stuffed his hands into his pockets and glanced at his truck, then at Emma's house, wondering what to do. He had two options: Drive around aimlessly by himself for a few hours or hang out with Kevin and Emma.

It was a no brainer.

His feet crunched the frozen, crusty grass, and his breath blew fog in his face. As Noah neared the house, muffled laugher and voices met him. Through the front window, he saw that Becky and Justin were already there, making themselves comfortable on Emma's sofa. Noah paused outside the door, knowing what would happen if he went inside. Becky and Emma would badger him about why he wasn't out for ice cream, and the topic of his dating life would take center stage once again.

But it was either that or aimless driving. So he knocked.

Kevin opened the door, and Noah ducked under his arm, holding out a staying hand to Becky and Emma. "Before either of you start in on me, I tried to call Cassie. But she wasn't home and hasn't texted back. So make some room. I'm staying."

"Good thing." Emma's eyebrows raised. "Because you're not dressed for a night out."

Noah glanced down at his Quicksilver t-shirt and comfortable jeans. What was wrong with the way he looked? There were no holes in the knees or paint stains that he could see.

"What's wrong with this?"

"Your jeans are okay," Emma conceded. "But your shirt is old and wrinkled, with a paint stain on the left shoulder."

He craned his neck. Oh. She was right. But it was just a little stain—hardly noticeable.

"And you really could use a haircut," added Becky. "Not to mention a shave."

Noah lifted his hands in surrender. "Anything else you'd like to criticize—I mean, point out?"

"Only that we're glad you're here," said Emma sweetly.

He rolled his eyes and sank down on a nearby chair.

There was a large bowl of popcorn on the coffee table, along with licorice and a bag of M&Ms. He grabbed a handful of the candy and tossed it in his mouth.

"So, what's it going to be?" he said as he munched. "Spades? Hearts? Rummy?"

"Uh . . ." Kevin slung his arm around Emma's back and pointed the remote at the TV. "You do know there's an elite eight game on tonight, right?"

"Elite what?"

Becky shook her head while Justin laughed. "Ever heard of March Madness? NCAA? Ring any bells?" Justin said.

Noah's expression cleared. "Oh, right. Isn't that some college basketball tournament?"

"It's *the* college basketball tournament." said Kevin. "And it's something we all plan to watch. Tonight. Together. Without cards."

Noah raised an eyebrow at his sister who was about as apathetic about sports as him. Or at least used to be, before Kevin's influence.

She shrugged. "He made me fill out a bracket this year, so believe it or not, I actually care who wins. Go Duke!" She made a fist pump in the air, then immediately put her hand to her stomach. "I think these little girls want them to win too."

"Boys. They're boys," corrected Kevin as he flipped through the channels, looking for the game.

"Girls," argued Emma. "Next week at our ultrasound, you'll see I'm right."

"Next week? Really?" said Noah. Where had he been?

Emma grinned and nodded.

"Men." Becky shook her head. "I've had that date marked on my calendar for weeks."

"Nobody told me," Noah said.

"Shh." Kevin cranked up the volume. "It's time for the tip-off."

Noah let out a breath and flopped against the back of

his chair, wondering how soon he could go home without interfering with the girls' night. It wasn't that he hated sports, he just didn't enjoy sitting around and watching them the way so many other people did. Growing up in third world countries hadn't given him many opportunities to play basketball or football, let alone watch them. And Angie hadn't cared for them either. It was only when the World Cup rolled around every four years that Noah sought out a game on TV.

The fact that Duke gained control of the ball right away did nothing for him.

Becky picked up her phone and read something. She grinned at Noah and pointed to it, mouthing, "Cassie."

Noah immediately pulled his phone from his pocket, noting with frustration that she still hadn't responded to his text. Did she even get it? Or was she ignoring him on purpose?

He chose to believe the former.

"What did she say?" Noah mouthed back.

Becky replied, but Noah couldn't make out the words.

"What?" he said.

"She wants a chick flick recommendation," Becky raised her voice. "What should I tell her?"

"Does that mean she's home?" Noah asked.

"Apparently."

"Oh, c'mon! How did you miss that?" Justin and Kevin simultaneously yelled at the TV, looking ready to strangle one of the players.

Time to go. If Cassie really was home, Noah suddenly had somewhere else he'd rather be. "Tell her to listen to music instead and work on her lyrics."

"What?" said Becky.

Noah answered with a grin. "Have fun watching the game," he called. "I'm out of here."

"Oh no, you don't," said Emma, struggling to get up. "Not until you change into one of Kevin's shirts."

"I'll second that," added Becky.

He hooked a thumb over his shoulder. "I'll just go home and—"

"No," they both said.

Giving up, Noah followed his sister down the hall. Hopefully, she wasn't planning to trim his hair too.

Ten

THE RING OF the doorbell echoed through the empty house, bouncing off the polished wood floors and satin gray walls. Cassie looked around, wishing there was soft, cushy carpet to absorb the sound and to sink her feet into. The new family room in the basement would have the plushest carpet she could find.

Adjusting the towel turban on her head, she grabbed the money off the counter to pay the delivery guy for the pizza she'd ordered earlier. It was her guilty pleasure, and one she had indulged in often since the funeral. Landon hadn't approved of carbs or cheese, but Cassie did. Very much so.

She pulled her front door open with a ready smile, but instead of the expected delivery guy, Noah stood before her. He looked amazing in a gray and turquoise plaid, button-down shirt and dark jeans. Cassie's smile froze as panic seized her heart. What was he doing here? She'd ignored his text on purpose.

Noah grinned at her. "I tried to text you earlier, but apparently you never got it because you didn't answer back."

He paused, watching her. "Or was it me who didn't get *your* reply?"

In each of his hands, he carried a bulging plastic grocery sack, containing small containers of . . . was that ice cream?

No, he didn't. He wasn't.

Cassie had no words—at least nothing she wanted to say out loud. Inwardly, she was shouting *I should have responded. I should have told him I was busy.* Then Noah wouldn't be standing on her doorstep, blaming the ignored text on unreliable technology.

"Anyway," Noah continued, apparently unconcerned that his question went unanswered. "I thought that instead of going out for ice cream, I'd bring it to you." He lifted the bags. "Assuming you're okay with it, that is."

Was there a polite way out of this situation? Cassie couldn't think of one. Should she be frank and tell him that she wasn't interested in going out with him or any other man? Ever?

Why didn't I just respond to his text? There was no one to blame but herself for this.

"Maybe it's a bad time," Noah said. "Would you rather not sample ice cream tonight? Nice towel, by the way."

Cassie's hands flew to the fluffy pink towel wrapped around her hair. She yanked it free and frantically raked her fingers through her hair, trying to restore some order to it. She opened her mouth to tell him that yeah, it was a bad time, but she couldn't make herself do it. He'd gone to all this trouble to bring her ice cream—and a lot of it, from the looks of it. The least she could do was let him come in for a few minutes.

She opened the door wider and nodded him inside. "What if I don't end up liking any of that ice cream?"

"Is that what you're worried about?" said Noah, scuffing his wet shoes against the mat. "If so, don't. There are millions of flavors out there. This is only the beginning."

The beginning? Beginning of what? It suddenly became

hard to breathe, and Cassie quickly decided she'd pick a favorite flavor tonight whether or not she actually liked it. This needed to be the beginning *and* the end. Especially the end.

She followed him down the hall and tossed the towel over one of the chairs in the kitchen.

"Where are your spoons?" Noah asked, pulling open one drawer after another. "Ice cream tasting is serious business. We can't contaminate any of the flavors, so you'll either need a different spoon for every flavor, or we'll have to rinse and dry."

Was he joking? "They're in the drawer by the dishwasher," she said before sinking down on a barstool and giving in to what was to come.

The doorbell rang again, and Cassie withheld a groan. Now what? It would be the pizza delivery guy for sure this time, and Cassie wasn't sure how she felt about adding a pizza to the mix. If she invited Noah to share it with her— something she couldn't exactly *not* do—it would only prolong the evening. But what other choice did she have? It wasn't like she could leave the poor kid standing in the cold on her front porch.

Cassie grudgingly moved to answer the door.

"Expecting someone?" Noah asked, his hand pausing on a half pried-open ice cream lid. For the first time since he'd arrived, he looked uncertain.

Well good, let him be the uncertain one for once. "Yeah, it's my date," Cassie said flippantly as she headed toward the door. "He's a little early."

"You're joking, right?"

Cassie smiled, not bothering to answer. *Serves him right,* she thought.

Moments later, she returned to the kitchen carrying a warm pizza box. She set it on the counter and cocked her head at Noah. "My hair is wet, and I'm wearing slippers. What kind of poor excuse for a date do you think I am?"

"You look great to me." He actually looked like he meant it.

Cassie shifted uneasily. Why did he have to be so nice? Or so full of it? "Says the guy who goes around wearing jeans with holes in the knees and paint-splattered t-shirts."

"Hey, I cleaned up tonight." He gestured at his clothes. "Check me out, not one drop of paint anywhere."

"Did you really just tell me to check you out?"

"That's right." He grinned, gesturing the length of his body. "Feast your eyes."

Cassie laughed—something she seemed to do every time he was around. Even in paint-speckled shirts, Noah was still handsome. And tonight, all cleaned up, he was heart-stoppingly so.

"You do look really . . . good." she admitted.

"Yeah, well don't be too impressed. My sister had to dress me." At Cassie's arched eyebrow, he quickly amended. "I mean . . . she didn't *dress me*, dress me. Just picked out a shirt for me to . . . uh . . . never mind."

Cassie laughed again. She couldn't help herself. This slightly awkward side to him was kind of cute—and so unlike Landon that it made Noah even more attractive.

"Your sister has good taste," she said.

He pointed a spoon at her. "Just so you know, I do know how to dress nice on my own."

"I'm sure."

He shook his head, as though mentally kicking himself for saying something stupid. Then he flicked a glance at the unopened pizza box. "So, are you, uh, in the mood for dessert first, or would you rather eat the pizza?"

Cassie pushed the box aside and sank back down on the barstool, clasping her fingers together. "I wouldn't want to 'contaminate' my palate with pizza, so I guess it'll be dessert first tonight. Besides, I'm dying to know who I really am."

He smiled and returned to prying off ice cream lids.

For the next twenty minutes, Cassie taste-tested each

flavor of ice cream. Noah made sure to keep all the names hidden so she wouldn't be "influenced" in any way. If she gave it a thumbs down, he'd let her see the flavor. But if it earned a thumbs up, he moved it to the Like lineup ordered from her favorite to her least favorite.

So far, Cassie had learned that she didn't like salted caramel or any version of chocolate ice cream. All the others, she really did like—but not enough to declare it a favorite.

And then she tasted something that had to be called Heaven on Earth.

"What is this?" she practically moaned, savoring the taste of mint, a hint of chocolate, and something else she couldn't place. "It's amazing."

She reached for the ice cream container, but Noah slid it farther away. "'Amazing,' as in goes to the top of the Likes pile? Or 'amazing,' as in *the one?*"

"The one, definitely," said Cassie. "What is it?"

Noah's lips twitched, and his eyes brimmed with mirth. "You sure you want to know?"

"Um . . . yes?"

He turned the carton around, revealing the flavor of mint cookie dough. The spoonful of ice cream Cassie had just eaten melted over her tongue and pooled on the bottom of her mouth. She swallowed, forcing the liquid down. "Oh, great. So I'm immature, too?"

"Not immature, Cass. Complex and interesting, remember?"

She chose to ignore that he'd shortened her name. Or the way it made her feel all mushy. "Don't forget doughy."

He laughed. "You're right. And doughy. But you like the mint version, which means you have an elegant and refined side to you. Whereas I . . ." his voice trailed off as though he had no idea how to describe himself.

"Are a little rough around the edges?" Cassie teased.

The corners of his lips quirked up. "Yeah. Rough around the edges. That's a good way of putting it."

It was becoming harder and harder to resist his charm. "This means I probably like the regular cookie dough ice cream too, doesn't it?"

He spun around one of the containers that she'd given a thumbs up to before. "You do, just not nearly as much. But maybe"—he shot her a meaningful look—"it will grow on you in time."

Cassie couldn't tell if he was talking about him or the ice cream.

"Maybe it will," she agreed, thinking of him. Though there were no maybes about it. He was definitely growing on her. And it scared her to death.

Cassie cleared her throat and set down her spoon, breaking eye contact. "If I don't stop eating right now, there won't be any room left for pizza." She tapped the box. "Want to share?"

"Depends. What kind did you order?"

"Pepperoni with black olives and peppers."

"Count me in."

Noah put the lids back on all the little ice cream containers and shoved them in her freezer, piling them on top of each other in a haphazard way. Cassie resisted the urge to nudge him aside and neatly reorganize them into rows and stacks—the way Landon had brainwashed her into thinking was the only way. But she stayed put, deciding that she liked them just the way they were. A little rough, like Noah.

As he pulled up the barstool next to her, his arm brushed hers, making her feel all mushy again. Cassie chided herself for enjoying the touch. And for wanting him to touch her again.

"Tell me about your family," she said.

As they shared the pizza, Noah complied, entertaining her with story after story of what it was like growing up in Africa and Central America. And with each story he told, Cassie felt her resolve to keep her distance crumble a little more. He seemed so genuine, so good. Was he for real? Or was he hiding his true self the way Landon had done?

"What about you?" he asked through a mouthful of pizza. "What's your family like?"

Cassie allowed a small smile to touch her lips. "Wonderful. And big. I have seven siblings, and they're all—"

"Seven? Are you serious?"

"Yes."

"Wow, what would that be like?" Noah shook his head in wonder.

"Loud, chaotic, crazy, and . . . pretty great." She paused, and her smile faded. "At least that's the way it was when I was growing up. It's been a while since I've done much with my family."

Noah watched her. "Don't you live close to them anymore?"

"Home is a twenty-minute drive from here."

When his eyebrows came together in confusion, she ran her fingers across the smooth, dark granite, wondering how to explain. "While we were dating, Landon loved our family parties, or at least he said he did. But as it turned out, he wasn't a fan of loud, chaotic, or crazy—unless it was with his friends. After we married, I was able to get him to come to a few things, then I went alone to a few things, and then not at all. I hated all the looks and carefully worded questions my parents and siblings asked. And it didn't help that it made Landon upset when I went. So I stopped."

Noah didn't look happy. "Even now?"

Cassie shrugged. "My mom calls about once a week to check in on me and invite me to Sunday dinner. And not long after the funeral, I went, thinking it would be just like old times, like I could get back to who I was before, you know?"

"But it wasn't?"

"No." Cassie's stomach clenched at the memory. "It was

awkward. Everyone tiptoed around me, as though they all knew my marriage had been a sham and didn't want to bring it up. My brothers didn't tease me the way they used to, the familiarity we'd once shared was gone, and my married siblings all have such great relationships with their spouses that it was a brutal reminder they'd chosen well. Whereas I . . . didn't. I hated that my presence made everyone else uncomfortable. So even though I still get invited and my parents and siblings continue to reach out to me, it's easier to stay away."

Noah watched her for a moment before asking, "Do you really believe that?"

She didn't want to, but . . . "Yes."

He leaned closer, resting his elbow on the counter. "Of course it's going to be awkward at first, but that will pass."

"Will it?" More than anything, Cassie wanted to believe him. But she was no longer the carefree girl from a few years ago. Things were so different now. She was different.

His hand came to rest on hers. "Yes, it will."

Her fingers stiffened, and she fought the urge to pull free.

Noah must have sensed her discomfort because he withdrew his hand. "Do I make you uncomfortable?"

Being put on the spot stunk. But Cassie didn't want to lie to him or pretend everything was hunky dory when it wasn't. "Truthfully? Yes."

"Why?"

She squirmed. It was one thing to admit something and another to explain it. "You seem like a really great guy, Noah. But you need to know that I'm not interested in a romantic relationship. I like having my freedom and independence, and I never want to give that up again."

"I would never ask you to give it up."

She looked at him. "But isn't that the nature of relationships? Sacrificing your wants for someone else's?"

"Well, sure. You definitely have to compromise sometimes, but—"

"That's just it." She swiveled on the chair to face him. "I don't want to compromise anymore. I like watching what I want to watch, wearing what I want to wear, going where I want to go, and being who I want to be. I like deciding on the layout of my basement, being able to choose carpet instead of hard wood or tile, and coming and going without having to answer to anyone. I never—ever—want to be married again."

Silence. Followed by, "I'm not proposing, Cass."

Great, now she was a drama queen. Her face infused with heat. "I know."

A small smile touched his lips, and he sighed. "Compromising *is* part of being in a relationship. But it's not a compromise unless *both* people give and take. How many times did Landon watch something that you wanted to watch? How much of the stuff in this house did he let you pick out? How many times did *he* sacrifice for *you*?"

Cassie bit her lip. Her marriage with Landon had been so lopsided. But did a relationship exist where both people felt they got as much as they gave? She wasn't so sure.

"That sounds so cut and dry when you put it that way," said Cassie. "But what happens if you clash over something big—something that can't be worked out with a compromise? Say one person wants kids and the other doesn't, or one person wants to move and the other person doesn't? Then what? When there's no way to meet in the middle, who loses and who wins?"

Noah pushed away the pizza box and leaned his arm on the island. "Is it really considered a loss to put someone else first?"

Cassie frowned. "I must be a horrible person because all the sacrificing I did for Landon never once brought me any amount of joy. Only resentment."

"That's because he was a taker. And takers take everything until there's nothing left to take."

A lump grew in Cassie's throat. That's exactly what Landon had been. A taker. "What about you?" she said. "Are you a giver or a taker?"

"Neither. I'm a compromiser."

But was he really? Cassie stood and began stuffing the leftover pizza into a plastic bag. "Was there anything big that you and Angie disagreed on?"

"Yeah," said Noah. "I wanted kids and she didn't."

In the middle of zipping up the bag, her fingers stilled. What sort of compromiser did that make him? She turned around and stuffed the pizza in her fridge, trying to dislodge that horrible lump. "So she was the one to give in on that."

Behind her, a barstool squealed against the floor and footsteps came closer and closer. Noah leaned a shoulder against the freezer door and waited until Cassie looked up at him.

"The reason she didn't want kids was because her career plans were more important, and she didn't want our children being raised in a daycare. She'd grown up in that situation and refused to do that to her own kids."

"Are you telling me she gave up her career, too?"

"No," said Noah. "I gave up mine."

The kitchen floor seemed to tilt, and Cassie had to press her palm against the refrigerator shelf to keep from tipping with it. Why did he keep doing this to her? It was like Noah was out to prove that good guys did exist and that he was one of them. But was he? Really? Was he the sort of guy Cassie wouldn't mind sacrificing for—someone she might actually *want* to sacrifice for?

No. No one was. She was happy exactly the way she was.

Cassie took a step back, putting some much needed distance between them. She started scrubbing spoons even though the dishwasher would have cleaned them.

Noah stayed where he was, but Cassie could feel him watching her. Studying her. Probably trying to figure her out the way she was trying to figure him out.

"Can I ask you a personal question?" he asked.

She scrubbed harder, feeling like this entire conversation had been personal. Too personal.

"Did Landon . . . uh . . . ever hurt you? Physically, I mean." The hesitant way he asked made it sound like he wasn't sure he wanted to know the answer.

The warm water ran over Cassie's hands for a moment before she finally shut off the faucet and faced him. Lines of concern and maybe even fear were etched across his handsome face. The room suddenly felt humid and stuffy, and her fingers pulled at the collar of her shirt.

"Once." Her voice was so quiet she could barely hear herself. She cleared her throat and said a little louder. "Only once."

"Only?" Noah's jaw clenched, and he looked away, his nostrils flaring slightly.

"Early on in our marriage, we got into an argument." She bit her lip. "It got pretty ugly, and I lost it. I accused him of not being the same man I married, and he slapped me, saying that I was the one who had changed—not him. My cheek was bruised for about a week. But after that, I learned to keep my opinions to myself, and things were . . . better."

"For him, maybe." The muscles in Noah's jaw twitched and moved. In his eyes, anger simmered. But it wasn't an anger that destroyed love and trust, like Landon's had done. It protected. It made her feel . . . safe.

Cassie returned to her scrubbing. Noah wasn't safe. No man was safe.

When the silence went from being comfortable to awkward, Cassie mustered a light tone. "Let's say you wanted to turn your basement into a playroom for the kids, and Angie wanted a home office. What would you have done then?"

Noah began loading the spoons in the dishwasher. "I would have turned the attic into the coolest playroom ever."

"What if you didn't have an attic?"

"Most houses have attics."

"What if it wasn't big enough?"

"I would find a way to make it big enough."

"But—"

"Cassie," he said, interrupting her. "If it had been me instead of Landon, I would have appreciated how important a dance studio was to you. And if there wasn't room for a playroom in the basement, and we didn't have an attic, I would have built a really cool playhouse out back. Or added on to the house."

She bit her lower lip, not liking her part in that scenario. "Then that would make me a taker."

"No." He closed the dishwasher with a snap and grinned at her. "You would have agreed to give me the garage for all my tools."

A small smile formed as Noah worked his charm yet again. "But where would I park my car?" she teased.

"I might be coerced into leaving enough room for your car."

She nodded. "Then I might be okay with that."

"See?" Noah's finger touched the tip of her nose. "We're not even dating yet, and we've already proved we can compromise. I'm pretty sure it's because we both like cookie dough ice cream. That makes us compatible."

All of his words blended together into one big run-on sentence. Except one. "Yet?" Cassie squeaked.

He winked. "Well, here's hoping anyway, assuming you'll actually respond to my calls or texts in the future."

The thought of being in a relationship with Noah filled Cassie with such conflicting emotions. It was a strange phenomenon, probably similar to the feeling of jumping out of an airplane. It was the thrill of the fall mixed with the petrifying realization that things might not turn out the way she hoped they would.

Before, with Landon, Cassie didn't fully comprehend the dangers. She didn't know chutes could malfunction or instability could cause midair injuries or throw off the landing. She'd been too preoccupied with the exhilaration of falling.

But now she knew better. Those few moments of bliss weren't worth the crash landing. They weren't.

Why, then, did she suddenly want to jump again?

"I'm scared, Noah," she admitted, her voice barely above a whisper.

His fingers brushed against her cheek in a wonderfully soft caress. "So am I, Cass. So am I. But I'm willing to risk it if you are."

With one last lingering gaze, he took a few steps back, then turned and left, leaving Cassie with warmth in her heart and a freezer full of ice cream.

Eleven

ALL CHATTER DIED when Noah walked inside. He found Sam, Becky, and Emma waiting on his couch with expectant faces. He wanted to groan. Or pull out his phone and send Justin and Kevin an SOS, begging them to intervene with their wives and daughter.

Not that they would.

"Well?" Sam, the most impatient of the trio, was the first to speak.

"Well what?" Noah dropped his keys on the side table and walked to the kitchen.

"What do you mean, 'Well what?' How was the ice cream?"

"Don't know. Didn't eat any."

Emma followed him into the kitchen, pausing next to the bar and folding her arms over her small mound of a tummy. "Noah, we've been waiting for you for an hour. I'm exhausted, and I'm sure Becky and Sam are too, and you have to be up early to hang drywall. So, how about giving us a break for once and telling us what happened without making us squeeze it out of you?"

Noah filled a glass of water and drank the entire contents in a long, drawn out chug. He set the cup on the counter. "Who won the game?"

"Noah!" all three girls called out in unison. Noah grinned. Teasing them never got old. Especially when it came to his sister.

"Please, bro, I'm begging you," said Emma. "We're only here because we love you and want to hear about your night."

He sighed. Emma did look exhausted. But that didn't make him want to talk about his night. "I know."

"I take it she let you in?" said Sam, plopping down on a barstool next to her mother. She set her elbows on the counter and dropped her chin into her palms.

Noah looked at the three faces before tossing his cup in the sink. "Okay, I'll give you the Cliff Notes version and that's it."

"We'll take it," said Emma.

"Assuming we can ask a few questions," Becky added.

"Yes, we most definitely need some time for Q&A." said Sam. "Wait, when did you change clothes? You look really good in that." Noah glared, and her mouth snapped shut. "Sorry. I'll be good and listen."

Noah leaned against the sink. "The only reason she answered the door was because she thought I was the pizza delivery guy. But, using my irresistible wit and charm, I convinced her to let me in and discovered that her favorite ice cream is mint cookie dough." He shot Becky a meaningful glance. "Then we shared a pizza, talked for a few minutes, and I came home. End of story."

From the looks on their faces, they weren't appeased.

"You did *not* talk for a few minutes," argued Sam. "You were gone for hours."

"Will there be a second date?" asked Emma.

"Not until there's a first," said Noah.

"Will there be a *first*?" said Becky wryly.

Noah nodded slowly. "That's up to her. If she says yes, then . . . yes."

Three happy, smiling faces appeared, and Noah took the opportunity to end the discussion. "Is it okay if we call it a night? Sam, thank you so much for watching the girls tonight."

"It's never a problem, you know that."

"I'm still grateful. They adore you."

"Of course they do. What's not to adore?" Sam said, making everyone snicker.

Noah watched them all file out the door, then went to check on his girls. Even though there were three bedrooms in the house, they still shared the fairy room that Emma had created years earlier. Noah had switched out the queen bed for two twins with picket fence style headboards that he'd made himself. Emma had painted them white with vines and flowers wrapped around them, then intertwined them with the little white lights that used to hang from their ceiling.

As usual, Adelynn was curled into a cocoon of blankets, and Kajsa was sprawled out on her stomach with her covers on the floor. Noah smiled and retrieved her blanket, spreading it over his daughter.

A pink scarf hung over the end of Adi's bed, reminding him of Cassie. Noah picked it up and sat down at the foot of her bed, playing with it between his fingers. Was he doing the right thing by wanting to go down the dating road again? Was Cassie a woman who could someday be more than just a dance instructor to his girls? Would they want her to be more? Would he?

Noah looked at the painting on the wall, the one of Angie and his girls that Emma had painted years earlier. He loved that picture. He loved that it reminded his daughters every day that they'd once had a beautiful mother who loved

94

them. Even though she hadn't been around much, Angie had adored her girls.

What would happen to that painting if he ever did remarry? Would Emma paint another to rest beside it, or would it be replaced? Noah didn't know. That would be up to the girls. All he knew was what he wanted to happen: that the memory of Angie remain beside the new memories that came from a new mother.

Whoever that turned out to be.

"I can't believe you talked me into this," Kevin grunted. His face was a deep red from the exertion of holding a large piece of drywall in place on the ceiling of Cassie's basement, while Noah drove in screws as fast as he could.

"I can't believe it either. If you had any common sense you would have turned me down," Noah said, knowing that Kevin wasn't the turning down type. He was too good of a guy for that. "Okay, you should be able to let go now."

"Whew." Kevin shook his arms and hands, reviving them, while Noah continued to drive in screws. "I also can't believe you actually like doing this."

Noah chuckled. "I don't. Drywalling is my least favorite part. But when it's done, and the room finally takes shape, it makes it all worth it."

"Even when it's someone else's room?" Kevin looked skeptical, or maybe he was just thinking of all the work that still needed to be done.

"Yes, even when it's someone else's room," Noah said. "As soon as you see the look on Cassie's face when she sees this all hung, you'll understand."

"I seriously doubt it."

Together, they reached for another sheet and hefted it above their heads, sliding it next to the one already in place.

Kevin splayed his arms and maneuvered his body toward the center of the board, keeping it in place, while Noah drove screws.

"Any news on the job front?" Kevin grunted, his face going red once more.

"I've gotten a few bites on my resume, but no offers just yet," said Noah, putting screw after screw in the drywall. With his magnetic drill bit, it didn't take too long. "Okay, it's good now."

Once again, Kevin let go and shook his hands. "Do you think you'll hear from your old company?"

"Already have. He's thinking he'll be able to hire me back near the end of the month—which will be about the time I finish this project. So hopefully everything will work out."

Kevin nodded, his expression thoughtful.

"What?" asked Noah.

"I was just wondering . . . have you ever considered starting your own company?"

Noah fiddled with a screw between his fingers before driving it into the drywall. "I've considered it, but I don't think I'm ready yet. The girls need stability—not the ups and downs that come with startups."

"As opposed to the steadiness of your past"—Kevin made quote marks with his fingers—"*stable* jobs?"

"Exactly," Noah grinned, even though Kevin was right. The nature of the construction industry was a constant flow of ups and downs. No matter what job he landed, there was never a guarantee that it would last. And if anyone did make him a guarantee—like his previous boss had done—there was always the contingency of "assuming we have the work." Which they hadn't.

"Seriously, what's keeping you from going out on your own? You've definitely got the skills, and you have the potential to make a lot more money."

That was just it. Noah had *the potential*—yet another

thing he couldn't guarantee. "The construction industry is incredibly competitive, and I don't have a name or the experience to land the kind of jobs I'd need to support a business. Besides that, the thought of running my own company freaks me out. I guess I'm not much of a risk-taker."

Kevin swiped his forehead with the back of his hand, leaving a trail of powdery white dust. "I can understand that. It's the reason I bought an existing practice instead of starting one on my own."

"So there you have it," said Noah.

"But," said Kevin, reaching for another drywall sheet. "If you ever change your mind, let me know. I'd be happy to help you out."

Noah gave him a wry smile. "Even if it includes hanging drywall every weekend?"

"I'd probably draw the line at that."

Noah laughed. "If I did ever start my own company, drywall is the first thing I'd contract out."

"Smart man."

They continued to work until the ceiling was completely covered with the muted gray sheets, minus the cut-outs for the can lights. Already the basement seemed larger, brighter, and more open. Cassie was going to love it.

While Kevin packed up the tools, Noah grabbed a broom and swept up the drywall scraps that had collected all over the concrete floor. As he worked, Noah listened for sounds upstairs. But there was no Irish music, no running water, and no overhead footsteps. Cassie hadn't even texted him about leaving the basement door open this morning. It had just been left open. Was she even upstairs? Or was she avoiding him again?

He'd put his money on avoidance. That's what scared people did. They avoided.

As Noah swept up the last of the scraps, he heard the faint sound of the garage door opening. He dumped the dustpan into the garbage sack and continued sweeping, even though it did little good. Kevin stood by the exterior basement door, checking something on his phone while he waited for Noah to finish up. Up above, a door closed and footsteps pattered lightly.

Noah held his breath, waiting . . . hoping . . . wondering . . .

"Are you going to tell her the ceiling is finished, or should I?" Kevin said dryly, apparently aware of the fact that Noah was lingering on purpose.

Noah leaned the broom against the wall. "No, we can go. She'll see it when she sees it, and I know you're anxious to get back to Emma."

One of Kevin's eyebrows lifted. "What about all that talk of the look on Cassie's face making it worth it? Are you really going to deny me my only reward for showering in drywall dust?"

"I really am." Noah brushed as much chalky dust from his hands and clothes as he could, all the while wishing another door would open, followed by footsteps coming down the stairs. But the sound of running water filled the silence instead.

It was time to go.

Noah headed for the door, stooping to grab his keys and drill case on his way out. Kevin watched him as he brushed past. "You sure you don't want to at least say goodbye?"

"I'm sure."

"You're the boss."

Noah reached for the doorknob at the same time the squeak of the upper basement door sounded. He froze, his heart thumping inside his chest. It was like he'd reverted back to his teenage years when the thought of talking to a girl made him anxious.

Light footsteps echoed down the stairs, and Noah brushed past Kevin again to meet her. But she wasn't looking at him, she was looking at the ceiling. Her beautiful eyes were wide with delight.

"You're finished already?" In her hands, she carried a pitcher of water and two glasses, which she handed off to Noah as she walked by, taking in all their hard work. She poked her head into the bathroom before walking through the short hallway to her future dance studio. "It looks so much lighter down here. This is so exciting! I can't wait until the walls get done."

Noah elbowed Kevin and shot him an I-told-you-it-would-be-worth-it look.

Kevin rolled his eyes and grabbed the pitcher of water from Noah, pouring himself a glass. "Should I leave you two alone?" he said under his breath.

Yes, go away. "Cass, this is my brother-in-law, Kevin. It's thanks to him we were able to get this done today."

"Yeah," said Kevin. "Noah had nothing to do with it. He sat around and watched me work the entire time." Kevin handed the pitcher back to Noah with a grin.

"I'm sure he did," Cassie said dryly. "But really, thank you both so much. It looks great."

Kevin gave Noah a brotherly side hug. "He's so great, isn't he? So, so great." He slapped Noah's back, and some of the water from the pitcher sloshed over the side and landed on Noah's dusty shoes.

He glared at Kevin, then glanced down at the gooey mess, resisting the impulse to dump the remaining water over his brother-in-law's head.

"Oh, that reminds me," said Cassie. "I figured you'd be hungry, so I picked up some sandwiches on the way home. They're upstairs in the kitchen. You can either eat them here or take them with you if you're ready to go."

"We'll stay," Noah said before Kevin had a chance to say otherwise. Then he shoved the pitcher into his brother-in-law's hands and followed Cassie up the stairs.

Noah had just taken a bite of his sub when Kevin said,

"Cassie, don't you think Noah should start his own company?"

Nearly choking on his sandwich, Noah shot Kevin a will-you-shut-up look.

Cassie set a glass of ice water in front of each of them. "Are you considering doing that?" she asked.

"No," said Noah.

"Why not? You're really good at what you do."

"Because it's risky. Because ninety-five percent of all startups fail within the first year. And because I don't want the added stress and hassle of owning a company." He paused. "As Kevin already knows."

"You own your dance company, don't you, Cassie?" Kevin said, ignoring him.

"Yes, but I think my situation is a lot different. I still work part time from home while I build my business, so it's not as scary for me. I can ease my way into it. And the business side of things isn't so bad yet either, though someday I hope to add some more teachers and locations. I love being my own boss, but I also appreciate the steady paycheck from my other job."

Noah set his sandwich down. "It would be a conflict of interest for me to start a construction company while working for another one, so easing my way into it isn't an option. I'd have to land a big job before I'd even consider it, and the likelihood of that happening is, well . . . highly unlikely."

"I get it." Kevin said, all humor gone. "I do. I just don't like seeing you go through layoffs every time business dies down. That's all."

Noah shifted in his seat, uncomfortable with the topic, especially in front of Cassie. In her eyes, he was probably the guy who couldn't hold down a job and the coward for not daring to go out on his own.

Why had he lingered in the basement again? Oh, right. Because he thought his brother-in-law had a filter.

"Maybe the impossible will happen, and you'll land that big job someday," said Cassie, her eyes sympathetic.

"Yeah." And maybe he'd become an astronaut and fly to the moon too.

Noah pushed his chair back and stood. It was time to cut his losses and get out of here. "Thanks for lunch, but we've got to get going."

Cassie nodded. "It was good to meet you, Kevin."

"You too. It's nice to finally put a face to the woman that Noah keeps going on and on about."

Unbelievable. Noah wouldn't be surprised if Kevin started chanting: *Noah and Cassie, sitting in a tree . . .* How old was his brother-in-law? Two?

It was definitely time to go.

"He's joking," Noah said to Cassie on his way out.

"He's right. I am," said Kevin. "Sort of."

Noah practically shoved his brother-in-law through the front door and waved goodbye. One step forward, ten million steps back. That's what today had been. And it was all thanks to a guy who Noah couldn't really be mad at because he'd just spent four hours of his time helping Noah hang drywall.

Twelve

CASSIE HUGGED HER arms to her chest as she watched Noah drive away. If he'd known the courage it had taken for her to open that basement door and invite them up for lunch, he would have been impressed. But now that he was gone, she wasn't sure if it was courage so much as stupidity.

He's a good guy.

Her heart yearned to believe it. Every time he was near, her pulse sped up, her heart danced, and her mind was put at ease. But the moment he walked away, doubts invaded like a loud *mayday*.

The scary fact was: Cassie didn't know Noah well enough to trust him yet, but the only way to get to know him was to spend more time with him. So she could either run like crazy in the opposite direction, or force herself to open that basement door and walk down the stairs.

Today, she'd chosen the stairs.

Why? The way she was feeling now, with her heart alternating between leaping and seizing, she didn't know what she was doing. Landon had only been gone nine months. Nine months! Cassie wasn't ready to start dating again and doubted she ever would be. She liked living on her own and being independent. She did.

But she'd also really liked dancing with Noah, eating ice cream with Noah, laughing with Noah, and thinking about Noah.

He was like a song that was stuck in her mind, replaying over and over again. *Noah, Noah, Noah.*

Cassie went to her room and threw herself onto her bed, burying her head beneath her pillow as she screamed at herself, at the world, and at Landon. When she had no more screams left in her, she rolled to the side and came face to face with a picture of her parents on her nightstand. They were sitting in the back of a Jeep holding hands and laughing. Cassie had snapped the picture during a family vacation to Cozumel when she was a junior in high school. Her mother's hair was a windblown mess, and her father didn't have much hair to speak of. And yet they adored each other. It was the kind of relationship Cassie had once yearned for with her future husband. The kind she didn't get.

But could she? Now? With Noah? Or was it just a pipe dream for her?

Cassie flipped onto her back and pulled her phone from her pocket. Unable to resist, she sorted through her text messages until she came to the ones sent by Noah. She reread them. She smiled. Her heart leapt. Hope flared.

She tapped Reply to the last message he'd sent.

I love my basement. Thank you for fixing my design and for taking the job. You're incredibly talented.

Her hand hovered over the Send button for only a moment and then it was gone. Her heart leapt and seized until his response came.

Thank you.

It was short and sweet, but it left Cassie feeling better. Maybe she'd made his day a little brighter the way he'd done for her so often. She set down her phone only to hear it chime again.

Speaking of your basement, want to go shopping for flooring next week? You need to make decisions on that soon.

Cassie stared at the message, trying to figure out what he meant. Was he telling her to go shopping on her own, or was he offering to go with her?

The chime sounded again.

It can be our first official date or just two friends picking out flooring. Your choice.

Cassie closed her eyes, trying to reconcile the trill in her heart with the warnings in her mind. The warning won out. With shaking fingers, Cassie took a deep breath and replied to the message.

Friends, she wrote.

He responded immediately. *Kissing friends?*

That made her smile. *Friends,* she wrote again.

Holding hands friends?

Friends.

Dating friends?

FRIENDS! She was laughing now.

Can't blame a guy for trying. Wednesday morning work for you?

I'm teaching a pre-Irish class that ends at 10:00.

11:00? I'll buy you lunch this time. From one "friend" to another.

A silly grin played on her lips. *K.*

Have a good rest of the weekend, Cass.

She loved how he took the time to add her name. *You too, Noah.*

Cassie set the phone down on the counter, a little in awe of the way his text messages had put her heart and mind in harmony with each other. In that moment, she felt peace, and it was a good feeling.

Her phone chimed again.

BTW, I'm sure your parents would love it if you dropped by for Sunday dinner.

And just like that, the spell was broken. Why had she ever confided in him about her family? If Noah ever offered to take her cliff jumping, Cassie would know better than to agree. He'd probably take her to the tallest cliff he could find, give her a nudge, and say, "Off you go."

The man apparently didn't believe in baby steps.

Even through her heavy coat, the bite in the early evening air made Cassie shiver. Warmth was only a few steps away, and yet she stood rooted on her parents' front porch, growing colder by the second.

Open the door and walk in, Cassie told herself, listening to the muted voices and laughter of her family. This was ridiculous. She'd been raised in this house. It was her home and always would be. Why, then, did she feel like a guest who should ring the doorbell and wait to be invited inside?

Maybe she *should* ring the doorbell.

An engine rumbled up to the curb behind her and then died. Cassie stiffened, knowing there was no way out now. Slowly, she turned around, surprised to see one of her sisters.

"Cassie? Is that you?" Tina shaded her eyes at the lowering sun, and her breath fogged up the air around her.

"It's me," Cassie said quietly, shivering again.

Tina had been the sister Cassie had been closest to growing up. They were three years apart, but they used to do everything together—at least until Tina had married and moved to Ohio. Cassie hadn't talked to her in over two years.

"You're here!" Tina rushed forward and threw her arms around her sister, hugging her tight. "I've missed you so much!"

"I've missed you too. What are you doing in town?" Colorado was a long drive from Ohio.

"Spring break."

"Oh."

Tina's husband gave Cassie a quick hug, then ushered two of their three children around the sisters toward the house. The third, he carried in an infant seat. Tina's children looked so old and tall, and now they had a new baby. Cassie watched them disappear inside. She'd missed so much over the past few years. Too much.

"I was going to drop by your house later tonight," said Tina.

"You were?"

"I know you're missing Landon—and you always will—but you can't keep pushing us away. You need us just as much as we need you, and I've had it. It's not right to feel like you don't even know your own sister anymore."

Of all her siblings, Tina was the most blunt and vocal of the lot—the type of person to step directly on something versus tiptoeing around it like the rest of her family. Maybe it was a good thing she was in town. Maybe easing back into "normal" wouldn't be so difficult with her here.

Assuming it was possible.

The front door opened, and Cassie's mother's voice rang out. "Cassie?" A smile stretched across her face. "You're here!" She rushed forward and enveloped her daughter in a hug while the rest of the family all gathered at the front door.

"I don't believe I know you, young lady," her dad spoke up next. "You look a little familiar, but I can't quite place your face."

"Oh, stop it." Her mother slapped him lightly on the arm.

But Cassie didn't want the teasing to stop. She wanted it to go on and on, wanted all of her siblings to join in. She wanted them to joke and tease and erase all the awkwardness that would inevitably come once the hugs and welcome homes had passed.

"I'm your sixth daughter and the baby of the family," said Cassie. "Ring any bells?"

"Well, whaddayaknow, the prodigal daughter has returned!" his voice boomed. "Should we kill the fatted calf?"

"Please no," said Cassie. "I'm now a vegetarian."

"What?" All humor gone, her father gaped at her. Not eating meat was a sin in his eyes.

Cassie nodded. "It's true. I only eat gluten-free bread, yogurt, and carrots."

"Shut up." Tina grabbed Cassie's hand and tugged her toward the house. "We all know you couldn't survive off of yogurt and carrots if your life depended on it. And gluten-free bread? Yuck."

"Believe it or not, it grows on you," said her brother,

107

Matt, apparently a fan of the bread. Cassie gave him a questioning look as she passed, and he shrugged. "Mel's allergic."

"You poor thing." Tina clasped her sister-in-law's hand as she passed. "I had no idea."

"Neither did we until a couple months ago," Mel said wryly. "But I feel a whole lot better since I went off of it."

"Now she's trying to get us all on a gluten-free diet," Cassie's other brother, Jake, muttered.

"Hey, all I asked is that you *try* the rolls," Melanie said.

"Who's dat?" a little voice called out. Cassie searched the room, pausing when she saw a little girl sucking her thumb while pointing the index finger of the same hand at Cassie. She looked about three or four. Which of her siblings had a daughter about that age?

Melanie crouched down, answering the question. "That's Aunt Cassie, sweetie."

"Aunt Caffy?"

"Yes, Aunt Cassie." Melanie gently removed her daughter's thumb from her mouth. "She's really nice."

"I don't know her."

"That's because you were sick the last time she came."

"I'm not sick."

"Not anymore. But you were . . . a while ago."

The room went silent, and Cassie's heart shredded. But she had no one to blame but herself. She shouldn't have stayed away so long. She shouldn't have stayed away at all. Cassie should have stood up to Landon and lived her life the way she'd wanted to. If she had, she wouldn't be standing in the middle of a tension-filled room, wondering how to explain to a sweet little girl why she didn't know her aunt.

Tina was the one to finally break the silence. "You don't know her yet, sweetheart. But you will." She shot a meaningful look Cassie's way. "Right?"

Cassie swallowed and nodded. "Right." She squatted in

front of the little girl and gave her a soft smile. "Like your mom said, I'm Aunt Cassie. What's your name?"

"Ella," she said, and her thumb went back in her mouth.

Ella had been toddling around the last time Cassie remembered seeing her. Now look at her. Walking and talking, with light brown hair so long she could have been named Rapunzel. "I hope we'll become very good friends."

Ella eyed her with skepticism. "I'm a dancer."

"Really? Me too. In fact, I teach little girls about your age how to Irish dance."

"Iwish?" Ella's expressive eyebrows drew together.

"Yes," Cassie said. "Maybe after dinner I can teach you a few skipping steps. Would you like that?"

Ella nodded slowly, then rewarded Cassie with a timid smile.

Cassie returned it and stood, feeling everyone's eyes on her.

"Since when did you start teaching dance?" Tina said in her blunt way.

"Aren't you still working for Hansen Imaging?" asked her mother.

Cassie let out a breath and looked around the room. She was tired of being the aunt her nieces and nephews didn't know or didn't feel comfortable around. She was tired of not knowing what was going on in her siblings' lives or if they were coming from Ohio for spring break. She was tired of keeping her distance. Tina was right. She needed her family. And maybe—hopefully—they needed her too.

"Yes, I'm still working for Hansen, but only part time. I also teach Irish dance in a small studio I'm leasing on the southwest side of town. But starting next fall, I'll be teaching in a brand new studio I'm having built in my basement with the hope that I'll be able to one day teach full time."

Talk of her new studio made Cassie think of Noah, and a warmth massaged her heart. There was no accompanying fear or anxiety, just a quiet, peaceful gratitude for his friendship and encouragement to come home. And though Cassie wasn't ready to tell her family about the guy who was finishing off her basement, she was finally ready to tell them the truth about Landon.

Thirteen

CARPET SAMPLES WERE way too small. How was Cassie supposed to know what an entire room would look like from a small little swatch? There were too many choices. Nylon or polyester? Plush, frieze, textured, or cut? Not to mention all the color options. And then there was the tile for the bathroom and the complicated dance flooring, with its subfloor and all of its choices.

She felt a headache coming on.

"How will I ever make up my mind?" Cassie whispered to Noah.

"It's called trusting your instincts."

"Instincts? I'm supposed to have an instinct about carpet samples?"

"Doesn't everyone?" Noah grinned. "Isn't one calling out to you? Telling you that it's the one you'll be able to coexist with for the next ten to fifteen years?"

Ten to fifteen years? Noah wasn't helping at all. Cassie frowned at the samples, willing one to shake or glow or whatever carpet samples did to call out to a person.

"Which one would you choose?" she finally said.

"Uh-uh. This is your house, your carpet, your choice. I'm just here as a *friend*, remember?"

A friend who was sitting way too close for comfort, Cassie thought as the touch of his shoulder sent a bunch of tingles down her arm. "Friends are allowed to give opinions."

"No. Only dates are allowed to do that," said Noah. "If you really want my opinion, you know what you have to do."

Despite her distress about all the decisions facing her, Cassie couldn't help but smile. "Okay, fine. It's a date. Now if you were me, what would you choose?"

Noah blinked as he shook his head. "Wow, that was easy. I should have gone for more. Like a kiss or boyfriend status or—"

She nudged him. "Stop it. I need you to help me, not tease me."

"I wasn't teasing," he murmured, pulling the samples toward him.

Cassie bit her lower lip to keep from smiling. Being with Noah was like opening the door to a gorgeous spring morning, with light, cheery blue skies, chirping birds, and the promise of warm sunshine. How could anyone shut the door on a day like that?

But wasn't that how she'd once felt with Landon? Cassie thought back, trying to remember. Dates with him hadn't included picking out carpet samples. They'd gone to movies, out to dinner at expensive restaurants, or hung out with his friends. Landon's flirting had been different too. More suave, sophisticated, and—looking back—not very genuine. It was like he'd memorized a bunch of lines, and Cassie had fallen for every single one of them.

Was she doing the same thing with Noah? Cassie watched him from the corner of her eye, wanting him to be real, to be the person he seemed to be. She was falling for that guy.

"Okay," he finally said. "What we need to do is narrow

this down. Is there a style you like better than another? Would you rather have this shorter, textured kind, or something more plush, like this?"

"Plush, definitely plush."

Noah tossed the textured carpets aside. "Do you want this stuff that looks and feels like a shaggy dog"—Cassie giggled—"or something more organized, like this."

"Well, since you put it that way. Organized."

Noah tossed the shaggy samples aside. "Shorter or taller?"

"Hmm . . . I'm not sure."

"Then we'll go with the medium length. How's that?"

Cassie nodded slowly, liking the look of the few remaining options. "Any of those are nice."

"Perfect. Now it comes down to polyester or nylon. Do you have a preference on that?"

"*Should* I have a preference?"

"Yes," said Noah. "Polyester is a little less expensive, but it will wear down over time. Nylon will hold its shape a lot better."

"Nylon it is."

"All right. Now all that's left is color." He pointed to an ugly hue of pinkish orange. "I'm assuming you want this one, right?"

It was awful, but Cassie nodded anyway, keeping a straight face. "I do like that one. It'll go perfectly with all my pink blankets and slippers."

The look on Noah's face said please-tell-me-you're-joking-because-I-was.

"Yes, that's definitely the one."

"Really?"

Her lips twitched. She couldn't remember the last time she laughed or smiled so much. Maybe never.

"What?" she said. "You don't think I should pick a carpet based on how well it matches my fuzzy, pink slippers?"

He shook his head and smiled. "If that's the way you want to pick out carpet, then go for it. Your house, your choice."

"In that case"—Cassie pointed to two different options—"it's between these two." One was a lighter color carpet with darker flecks in it, and the other was slightly darker.

Noah looked them both over and nodded. "I don't think you could go wrong with either of those."

"They pass the friend test?" she asked.

"No, they pass the date test," Noah corrected. "I've been upgraded, remember?"

Cassie laughed again, and before she could think twice about it, she stood and held out her hand. "C'mon, let's go decide on the studio flooring."

Without hesitating, Noah accepted her hand and immediately interlaced his fingers with hers. Warmth and shivers and happiness filled her, leaving very little room for anxiety. Noah Mackie was nothing like Landon Ellis. And for the first time since meeting Noah, Cassie let herself begin to believe it.

Noah drove slow on purpose.

For someone who claimed to not know her own mind, Cassie had made record fast decisions on all the flooring for her basement. Really, all she'd needed was someone to narrow her options down and explain the pros and cons of each. Noah had hoped it would take a little longer, but now here they were, back in the truck and on their way home with an entire hour and a half before Adelynn and Kajsa got off the bus.

He shouldn't have been quite so efficient at helping her out.

She'd lowered her guard today, which had been an unexpected surprise. But Noah worried that as soon as time and distance came between them, it would go right back up. Trying to get her to open up was like trying to straighten a spring. The moment he let go, she recoiled.

"Every Breath You Take" by The Police came on the radio, and Cassie turned up the volume. "I don't really care for the lyrics, but I love the beat of this song," she said.

Her beautiful, clear voice filled the cab of his truck as she sang. Noah didn't join in. He just listened, thinking of how his girls would love to hear that voice sing them a bedtime song.

"I'm a pool hall ace," Cassie sang. "'With every breath you take.'"

Pool hall ace? Was that what she'd said? Noah threw his head back and cackled. She immediately stopped singing and turned down the volume. "Oh no, I sang the wrong words again, didn't I?"

"I don't know." He flashed her a grin. "Did you say, 'I'm a pool hall ace'?"

"Um . . . no?"

"Then what?"

"I said . . . something different than that."

He couldn't stop laughing. She was hilarious. "Let me guess. You said, *'How my poor heart aches.'*"

"Right. That's exactly what I said. 'How my poor heart aches.'" She shook her head and looked out the window. "I guess that does make more sense."

"You guess?" He lifted her hand and kissed it. "You make me laugh."

"At least I'm good for something."

More than ever, Noah didn't want to drop her off anytime soon. Would it be too much to invite her to dinner? Would his girls mind if they got off the bus and found Ms. Cassie at their house? Would Cassie even accept?

Probably not.

The light in front of them turned red, and Noah slowed to a stop. Across the way, sunlight glinted off the door of what appeared to be a small furniture shop on the corner. A nightstand sat inside the front window, refinished with cream paint and an antique glaze.

Antique. Hmm . . . Cassie liked antiques.

When the light turned green, Noah drove forward, then made a U-turn. "What do you say we check out that store?" He pointed. "Maybe we can find something you could use for a vanity inside."

"Okay."

He parallel parked at the curb, and they both walked inside. Bells jingled, and the smell of musk, oil, and a hint of vanilla met them.

"May I help you?" said a petite woman at the counter. Long, dangling earrings swayed from her ears, nearly touching the woman's shoulders.

"Just browsing," said Noah.

She nodded and returned to the book she was reading.

Noah led Cassie past rustic coffee tables, wooden rocking chairs, and a stack of headboards piled against the wall. He was more interested in the dressers he saw near the back.

"I don't see any vanities," said Cassie, her finger making a path through the dust on some of the pieces.

"You don't really need an actual vanity." Noah released her hand so he could push a few things aside to get a better look at them. "With a few modifications, a chest of drawers or credenza could easily be converted into one. This one, for example, could work just fine." He studied the distressed cherry dresser, thinking of how he could remove the top drawer, give it a fresh coat of paint, and turn the old relic into something nice and antique-ish. "What do you think?" He glanced over his shoulder at Cassie.

She pressed her lips together, cocked her head to the side, then shook her head. "It's not my favorite."

"Is there anything here you do like?"

She turned around and began browsing, fingering knobs on some and trim work on others. She finally paused in front of an actual vanity in the far back corner and bent to open the two cabinet doors.

The size was right and the dark finish on the black walnut beautiful, but that was all it had going for it. Hand carved designs spiraled up the legs, and intricate, garish scrollwork ran across the top and bottom, with even more trim around each cupboard door. It was like the carpenter had crammed all of his ideas and designs into one design.

There was no way Cassie would seriously consider something like that, would she? No, this was another one of her I-like-pink-carpet jokes.

She glanced over her shoulder. "I think this one has potential, don't you? Though I'd want to refinish it with a lighter color."

A lighter color? No way. The over-the-top detailing would look even worse, if possible. His lips twitched. "I think you should paint it pink."

Her eyebrows scrunched together. "Pink? No, I was actually thinking of making it look more like that nightstand in the front window. The cream color one with dark edges."

Noah searched her face for any sign of humor. But her lips didn't twitch, her eyes didn't crinkle, and that adorable dimple remained hidden. But she couldn't be serious, could she? There was a reason that nightstand was in the front window instead of that vanity. A very good reason.

"Do you think it would look good?" she asked.

The back of Noah's head suddenly felt itchy, so he scratched it instead of answering. If only she'd crack a smile or something—anything to show him she was joking.

Instead, she took a few steps back, cocking her head to the side once more. "I like that there's nothing contemporary about it. And I love that Landon would have hated it." She looked at Noah. "Seriously, what do you think?"

So she *wasn't* joking. Wow. No wonder Landon had wanted to pick out everything in their house. If this was what her tastes were like . . . wow. The back of Noah's neck suddenly felt like ants were crawling all over it. He hated being put on the spot, especially when it came to her. How in the world was he supposed to sugar coat "I can't stand it"?

Nothing came to mind, so he remained silent and continued to rub his neck.

"You hate it," she said, watching him.

"I wouldn't say 'hate,'" he finally hedged, dropping his hand to his side.

"What would you say then?"

That it's hideous and gaudy beyond all reason. "That if you really like it, you should get it." Though he couldn't imagine her not coming to regret the purchase, especially the first time something spilled down the front of the cabinets and she had to try to clean it out of all those little nooks and crannies.

"But you don't like it," she said.

"It's not about what *I* like, it's about what you like."

"What don't you like about it?" Her eyes searched his, curious. "I really want to know."

Not knowing what else to do, Noah shoved his hands into his pockets and shrugged. "Well, don't you think it's kind of . . . I don't know, kitschy?"

The expression froze on her face, making it impossible for Noah to even guess what she was thinking. Had he offended her? Probably.

Maybe he needed to explain his opinion a little better. Noah sighed and gestured to the cabinet. "First of all, that's black walnut, and it would be a sin to cover it up with paint. Secondly, whoever crafted this piece, while talented, obviously didn't know when to quit. There's way too much detailing, and I think you'd come to hate it after a while. And thirdly, you should never buy something just because it's the opposite of what Landon would have liked. He's gone and will never see it. You, on the other hand, will have to live with it every single day."

Noah clamped his mouth shut, realizing he'd probably been a little too blunt. Then he rushed on to say, "But if you really like it, then get it."

Her eyes widened before she uttered a laugh—a strangled sort of laugh that didn't sound humorous at all. "Like I'm really going to get it now. C'mon, let's go."

Great. He *had* offended her. Noah quickened his steps and reached for her arm, pulling her to a stop. "Cass, if you didn't want my opinion, why did you ask for it?"

She glared at him. "Because I didn't think you'd make me feel like my tastes belonged in . . . in . . . Oscar's garbage can."

What? "Oscar who?

"The Grouch?"

Noah blinked. What was she talking about?

"Unbelievable." Cassie shook her head and pulled her arm free, moving toward the door.

Noah followed, catching up to her in the front of the store. "Cassie, stop. I'm sorry, okay? I honestly didn't mean to make you feel like that. It just sounded like the only reason you like that vanity is because it's something Landon would have hated. And that's not a reason to like something."

She was still glaring. "That's only one of the reasons I like it. I also happen to think it has a lot of charm and character."

"Then get it!" Good grief. Why were they even arguing about this?

Cassie's chest rose and fell several times before she finally looked him in the eye and lifted her chin a notch. "You know what? I think I will."

"Great."

"I agree. It is great." She stalked up to the counter and faced the girl with the long earrings. "I'm interested in the black walnut vanity in that far back corner. What's the best price you can give me on it?"

The girl glanced over her shoulder. "You're in luck. We've had that piece forever, so I can give you fifty percent off."

"Fabulous. I'll take it."

Noah clenched his teeth to keep from pointing out that there was a reason the vanity had been there forever.

Once it had been paid for, Noah helped the clerk load it on a dolly and cart it out to his truck. He strapped it in with tie downs, then slid in next to a stone-faced Cassie. His key was in the ignition before he let out a breath and turned to look at her. Whatever he was about to say died on his tongue when he saw a single tear trail down her cheek. She quickly swiped it away and looked out the passenger window.

Noah suddenly felt like the world's biggest jerk.

"Hey," he said, reaching out to her. "I'm sorry. I didn't mean to make you angry."

She sniffed but didn't move when he touched her shoulder. "I'm not angry. I just hate feeling like my opinion is wrong or stupid."

"Is that what you thought I was doing? Because I didn't mean . . ." Well, in a way, he sort of had. Unintentionally.

Her throat moved as she swallowed, and her gaze remained fixed on the window. "I don't think you did it on purpose, the way Landon used to do. But it still . . . hurt."

Noah turned to face her. "Cassie, what did you want me to say? You asked for my opinion, and, admittedly, I could have been a little less blunt, but I was honest. Would you rather I'd have lied and said I liked the vanity when I didn't?"

She shook her head and sniffed again.

"Then what?"

"I don't know." Her voice was so quiet Noah could hardly hear her. "Do you mind taking me home now?"

Noah nodded and started the car. In silence, they drove back to her house. What had started off as such a fun and lighthearted day had twisted into something that Cassie would probably use to keep him at a distance from here on out. Noah didn't want that. He wanted to continue to get to know the real her—the one buried beneath her pain and hiding behind all the walls. But if that's where she preferred to remain, he couldn't drag her out forcefully. It had to be her choice.

Her choice.

He pulled to a stop in front of her house and shut off the engine. Cassie helped him carry the vanity to her garage, where they left it in the middle of the second bay, looking even more garish next to the plain and pristine white walls of her garage.

"Thank you," she said.

"No problem." Noah fished his keys from his pocket and turned to leave. He hadn't taken more than two steps when she called his name. He turned back, waiting and hoping she'd say something to take away the sick feeling in his gut.

"What you said back there—about me choosing the vanity because it's something Landon would have hated—well, you were right. That's probably the real reason I do like it. But is that so wrong? Is it wrong to wear pink because it was his least favorite color? Or wrong to have a taste aversion to eggs Benedict because that was his favorite breakfast?" Her wide green eyes pled with his, and Noah felt a tug on his chest.

He pulled her into a hug. At first, her body was stiff, but then she melted against him, wrapping her arms around his waist and burying her face into his chest.

"No, Cass. It isn't," he murmured, breathing in the fruity smell of her shampoo. His chin came to rest on the top of her head as he held her. She felt so good against him. So right. Unable to resist the temptation, his fingers combed through the ponytail that cascaded down her back. Her hair was soft and silky, just like her hands. She was so alluring, so beautiful, so . . . vulnerable.

She lifted her gaze to his, and suddenly all Noah could see was Cassie. Her warm green eyes with tiny flecks of gold, the strands of light, strawberry hair that had escaped her ponytail, the mole to the side of her right eye, the freckles that speckled her cheeks, and her lips. She was beautiful. More than anything, he wanted to kiss her.

Would she let him?

Tentatively, Noah touched the strands of hair, brushing his fingers lightly across her high cheekbone as he tucked them behind her ear. Instead of pulling away, she pressed her fingers into his back, encouraging the closeness.

Noah dropped his forehead lightly against hers. Their breaths collided and mingled as his chest rose and fell. Cassie pushed up onto her tiptoes and let her cheek touch his. Her breath on his neck sent chills down his spine. Cautiously, his hands travelled down her arms to her fingers, and his lips brushed against her soft neck.

She shivered and leaned into him.

Behind Noah, a car pulled into the driveway, and Cassie was out of his arms before Noah had time to even think of a curse. Footsteps approached from behind, and Cassie eyed the intruder with a wary expression. "Tina. What are you doing here?"

Noah turned around and met the woman's gaze. She had long, curly dark hair, high cheekbones, and the same green eyes as Cassie. A sister, maybe? She watched Noah with a cool distrust before her attention finally returned to Cassie. "Mom sent you a text earlier, but you never responded. So I said I'd drop by to make sure you got it. Something came up with Dillon's work, and we have to leave tomorrow instead of Saturday, so everyone is invited over for dinner tonight if you want to come."

"Oh, sorry." Cassie snatched her purse off the roof of her car and rummaged through it for her phone. She quickly scanned her messages. "I didn't hear it ring. Yes. Of course I'll be there."

An awkward silence followed until Tina finally said, "Well? Are you going to introduce me?"

"Oh. Yes." Cassie slung her purse over her shoulder and gestured to Noah. "This is Noah. He's a good friend of mine who's helping me with my basement. And this is Tina."

"A friend, huh." Tina eyed him once more, her expression more speculative than curious.

"Actually, I'm her date," Noah corrected. "Right, Cass?"

"Seriously, Noah?" Cassie said. He could hear the eye roll in her voice. A light blush reddened her cheeks, and he grinned.

"Seriously."

"And I'm her older sister," said Tina, bringing the attention back to her.

Noah held out his hand. "Good to meet you, Tina. I've heard a lot about you and the rest of your family."

Her handshake was strong and confident. "Wish I could say the same about you."

"He was kind enough to go shopping with me this morning," blurted Cassie. "We picked out a vanity for the new bathroom in the basement. What do you think?"

Noah didn't appreciate her use of "we." He wanted no credit for anything involving that vanity. Especially not the picking out of it.

Tina's eyes widened when she saw the piece, and not in a good way. "You're not really going to put that in your basement, are you?"

A snicker escaped Noah's mouth, which earned him a glare from Cassie. "Yes, I am," she said. "I happen to like it."

"Only because Landon would have hated it," Noah felt the need to explain.

"Ah," said Tina, nodding slowly. "In that case, I think I like it too."

"Really?" Cassie asked.

"It's gorgeous."

"Thank you." A genuine smile spread across Cassie's

123

face, and Noah could have hugged Tina for putting it there. Even the vanity looked a little less gaudy. Sort of.

Noah could only hope Cassie got over her hatred of all-things-Landon-would-have-liked before it came time to pick out her family room furniture.

"So . . ." Tina was back to studying Noah, this time with an open curiosity. "Tell me, Mr. Friend-who's-now-a-date, would Landon have hated you too?"

"He would have loathed me," said Noah. "Despised. Detested. Abhorred . . ."

Cassie laughed, and a tiny smile lifted the corners of Tina's mouth. "Why?" she asked.

Apparently, Noah was being sized up and grilled, which was fine with him. He liked Tina. She was blunt, no nonsense, and apparently very protective of her little sister. He admired that. He just had no idea how to answer the question.

"Because I like cookie dough ice cream," he finally said.

Cassie snickered, and Tina arched an eyebrow. She looked so much like Cassie in that moment, that Noah couldn't help but like her more.

"That means he's complex, interesting, and a little doughy." Cassie's eyes were bright with the humor of an inside joke.

"Exactly," Noah agreed.

Cassie turned back to her sister. "He's like that vanity."

"Pardon?" Noah's smile immediately disappeared. Being compared to cookie dough ice cream was one thing; the vanity another.

It was Tina's turn to snicker. "You're a little on the ostentatious side too?"

"No." He was nothing like that vanity. Not even in the same universe as that vanity.

"I meant he's nothing like Landon," said Cassie, linking her arm through Noah's in a protective gesture. She looked up at him, and in her eyes he saw admiration, warmth, and a confidence that melted away any offense he'd taken at being compared to a gaudy piece of furniture. Somehow, Noah had earned some of her trust. He didn't know how or when, but he had. And he'd take it.

Then another thought occurred to him. When Cassie's Landon-hating blinders came off and she came to her senses about that vanity, would she come to her senses about him too? He hoped not.

He glanced at his watch, relieved to see that his girls would be home soon. "Sorry, but I need to run."

Cassie nodded. "Will I see you tomorrow?"

"I'll be the guy covered in drywall mud in your basement."

"Can't wait." Her eyes widened when she realized what she'd said. "I mean, I can't wait for the basement to get done."

"That was a Freudian slip if I've ever heard one," muttered Tina, making Cassie duck her head and a goofy smile appear on Noah's face.

Taking a few steps back, he said, "I'm glad you dropped by, Tina. It was nice to meet a member of Cassie's family."

"I'm sure everyone else will be anxious to meet you as well." She looked pointedly at her sister. "Which will be when, by the way?"

Without waiting around for the answer, Noah strode to his truck, leaving the two sisters to sort things out in the garage.

The goofy smile stayed on his face the entire way home.

Fourteen

PINK AND BLUE helium balloons decorated the entire ceiling in Emma's front room, with coordinating pink and blue streamers swirling and cascading down all around. It was a really cool sight—one that had Adelynn and Kajsa transfixed.

"Can we do this for my next birthday?" Adelynn asked in hushed tones.

"Mine too," added Kajsa, whose birthday was only two months away. "Only I don't want pink. Just blue and orange."

Noah ducked his way through all the streamers, eventually finding his sister in the kitchen, putting the finishing touches on white frosted cupcakes with crystal sugar sprinkles. "Way to go, sis. You've now set a new precedence for birthdays. Kajsa and Adi are already planning a helium balloon extravaganza."

"Isn't it pretty?" Emma said. "I rented a helium tank, and Becky and I went to town this afternoon. It was fun."

"Yeah, you guys definitely went to town." He leaned forward, resting his elbows on the counter. "So . . . want to tell me which color we'll be popping?" Emma's ultrasound appointment had been earlier that day. Her plan was to make the announcement, then give everyone a pin and let them pop whichever color didn't apply. The remaining balloons would be set free in the sky as a tribute to her unborn babies.

"Nuh uh." She wagged a finger at him. "Not yet. You'll have to wait until everyone gets here."

"Good luck telling Kajsa and Adi that."

The girls burst through the streamers, eyes glowing with excitement. "Are they boys or girls?"

Emma gave them a playfully stern look. "Is Uncle Kevin home from work yet?"

Their expressions fell. "No."

"Is Aunt Becky or Uncle Justin here yet?"

"No."

"Can you see Sam and Grandma and Grandpa Grantham on FaceTime yet?"

"No."

"Then do you really think I can tell you that?"

"No." They sounded so glum that Noah laughed.

Emma leaned across the island as far as her protruding tummy would allow. "Will two cupcakes cheer you up?"

"Really? Before dinner?" Wide-eyed, Adelynn looked at her father for permission.

"Go ahead," he said. "This is a special occasion."

"Yay!" Adi went for a pink one while Kajsa snatched up a blue. Adelynn delicately removed the wrapper from hers, and Kajsa ripped hers off before taking a large bite.

"Kajsa, really?" said Adelynn, her tone one of rebuff.

"What?" Kajsa said through a mouthful of cupcake.

Noah chuckled, and Emma came around to kiss the tops of both their heads. "My babies are going to have the best babysitters in the world."

Not long after, they heard the garage door open and

Kevin's voice call through the mass of balloons. "Holy cow, Emma. Where did our house go?"

The girls giggled, and Emma smiled. When Kevin emerged, he pulled his wife into his arms and kissed her soundly. "I should have known you couldn't keep it small," he murmured. "It looks awesome."

"I can't wait to tell everyone our news."

"I'm impressed you've kept it a secret this long."

"It hasn't been easy."

Kevin excused himself to change and get the grill started while Emma finished frosting the cupcakes. The girls helped with the sprinkles, and Becky and Justin arrived soon after, carrying a salad and rolls.

"Can you believe she's making me wait, too?" Becky said to Noah the moment she saw him.

"For good reason," said Noah. "I'm her brother. I should know first."

"Yes, but I was the one over here helping her blow up all those balloons this afternoon. Where were you?"

"Working."

"On what? How to get Cassie to date you? I thought you spent the day shopping with her."

Noah glanced at his girls who were too busy playing with the balloons to pay attention. He dropped his voice. "Trying to get Cassie to date me *is* work. She's not making it easy."

"Good for her." Becky grinned. "But I still think I should get to know Emma's news before you."

"In your dreams."

"How old are you two?" Justin said, stealing a cupcake. "Emma will tell *all of us* when she's good and ready so stop bickering."

"Thank you, Justin," said Emma.

Becky swatted his arm. "Honey, you're supposed to be on my side."

"I am on your side," he said. "Your left side, to be

exact." He was rewarded with a laugh from Noah and another swat from his wife.

After they'd eaten dinner, Sam's call was the first one to come through on Emma's iPhone. Kevin then called his parents, and as soon as everyone was listening in, all eyes turned to Emma and Kevin.

She cleared her throat and announced. "I guess now's the moment you've all been waiting for." A pause and then Emma elbowed her husband.

"What?" he said.

"Drumroll. I need a drumroll."

"Do I look like a drum to you?"

"Dum dada dum!" Noah said before the argument could go any further.

"Thank you, Noah," said Emma. Then she turned to the group and raised her voice. "Okay, so *now* is the news you've all been waiting for. Today, we learned that I was right." She paused, then squealed, "We're having a girl!"

"*And* a boy," added Kevin. "Which makes me right too, though she'll never admit it."

Suddenly, everyone was talking and congratulating them at once. Kisses were blown on FaceTime screens, hugs were given, and happiness filled the spaces in between.

It wasn't until all the excitement died down that Kajsa finally said, "Does this mean we can't pop any of the balloons?"

"It means we get to let them all go," said Emma. "Won't that be cool?"

"Is it okay if I keep a few?" Adelynn asked, her fingers tangled in several streamers.

"I have a better idea," said Emma. "Why don't we let all of these go, then you and Kajsa can make as many balloons in as many colors as the remaining helium in the tank will allow. I bought some multi-colored packs just for you."

"Thanks, Aunt Emma!" Adelynn hugged Emma's expanding waist, and Kajsa followed suit. Once Emma had freed herself, she opened both sides of the French doors leading out to her backyard, and everyone gathered as many balloons as they could carry, forcing them outside. The chilled air felt good after being in a room filled with bodies and balloons.

"Five, four, three, two, one, go!" Over a hundred pink and blue balloons floated into the sky, rising up as one giant, colorful mass, then gradually separating and growing smaller and smaller. The girls ran around to the front to see if they could get a better view, but Noah stayed where he was, thinking of his own daughters, of heaven, and of Angie. He still missed her smile and the confidence that came so easy to her. He missed their late night conversations and the closeness they'd once shared. Was she looking down on them now and watching over her family? Did she see the beautiful young girls that Adi and Kajsa were becoming? Did she agree that they needed a mother?

What do you think, Ang? Would Cassie be a good mother?

A pink balloon danced away from a small grouping, tossing and twirling in the wind and reminding Noah of the way Cassie danced. A pleasant sensation registered in his heart and spread through his body, warming him. Yeah, he thought so too.

Fifteen

THE WIND HISSED and howled outside, causing the door of the dance studio to shudder and shake. It was a sound that belonged in late October, along with jack-o'-lanterns, creepy costumes, and cackling—not the sound Cassie wanted to hear in early spring. She placed her palm on the door to still the vibrations and squinted through the late snowstorm for headlights. But all she saw was a swirling mass of white mixed with gloomy gray clouds.

Where are you, Noah?

All of the other parents had come and gone, and Adelynn and Kajsa had already removed their ghillies and were now sitting on the chairs, waiting for their father. Through the reflection in the glass, Cassie could see the worried lines across their foreheads and feel them on hers. Noah had been late before, but never *this* late.

Maybe she should call to make sure he was okay.

Cassie snatched up her phone and noticed he'd sent a text nearly an hour earlier. It must have come through during class.

My old boss called and wants me to drop by for a bit. I might be a few minutes late picking up the girls. Is that okay?

Cassie quickly responded.

Sorry, only just got this. And yes, it's fine. Take as long as you need.

His response came through moments later.

Taking a little longer than I thought. Sorry. Be there as soon as I can.

Drive safe.

Relieved that he wasn't stranded on the side of the road somewhere—or worse—Cassie set the phone down.

"Your dad just texted. He'll be here soon. But in the meantime, how about we play a little game?"

Adelynn nodded, but Kajsa looked skeptical. "What kind of game?"

"Definitely not one that involves Irish dancing," said Cassie with a smile.

Kajsa smiled back. "Okay."

Cassie pulled a chair around and sat in front of the girls. "Okay, so we need to come up with a category for the game."

"What do you mean?" Adelynn asked.

"Oh, you know. Like countries, ice cream flavors, animals—"

"Animals. Let's do animals," Kajsa said.

"Animals it is." Cassie scooted her chair a little closer. "How about we start with you, Kajsa? You say the name of an animal, then Adelynn and I will have to think of another animal that starts with the last letter of the one you say. Make sense?"

They nodded.

Kajsa didn't waste any time. "Horse," she said.

"Okay." Cassie looked at Adelynn. "Now your turn. What's an animal that starts with an E?"

"Elephants."

"Good," said Cassie. "Now my turn. Hmm . . . an animal that starts with an S . . . Oh, I know. Sheep."

"Pony," said Kajsa.

A few seconds later, Adelynn chimed in with, "Yak."

Wow, these girls were good. "Koala," said Cassie, wondering how fast Kajsa would be with the letter A.

"Andalusian."

"Anda-what?" Adelynn said exactly what Cassie was thinking.

"Andalusian," repeated Kajsa. "It's a kind of horse."

Adelynn rolled her eyes. Then she scrunched up her adorable little face, presumably thinking of an animal that started with N.

Good luck with that, Cassie thought.

Her expression finally brightened. "Nemo!"

"That doesn't count," said Kajsa.

"I think it does," said Cassie. "Very creative, Adi."

Adelynn shot her sister a triumphant, so-there sort of smile.

"My turn," announced Cassie. "Hmm . . . an animal that starts with an O." The first animal that came to mind was an ox, but Cassie immediately dismissed it, not wanting to stick Kajsa with an X. Instead, she said, "Octopus."

"Shire," Kajsa announced.

Adelynn groaned. "Is that another horse name?"

"Yep."

The chair squeaked as Adelynn flopped back. "All Kajsa reads about is horses. She's *obsessed*."

Cassie was starting to figure that out. No wonder Kajsa always wore the same faded and tattered sweatshirt with the horse galloping across the front. The little girl loved horses.

Not Irish dance. Horses. Why hadn't Cassie figured that out before?

"Have you ever ridden a horse, Kajsa?" she asked.

Her expression fell. "Only a pony at a fair one time. It didn't go very fast."

"Daddy says real riding lessons are too expensive," Adi added.

"They are expensive," Cassie agreed. "It takes a lot of money to care for them."

"I know." Kajsa kicked at her ghillies on the floor, looking dejected.

Cassie's heart went out to the girl who showed up every week for lessons she wasn't thrilled about. A little girl who was so sure her dreams were beyond her reach.

But they weren't. Not really. If Cassie lowered her pride and opened yet another door she'd closed after meeting Landon, she could make them come true.

"You know, Kajsa," Cassie said. "I have a wonderful uncle who happens to own a ranch. The last time I was over there"—*over two years ago*—"I noticed they had a lot of horses. Maybe one of these days, if your dad says it's okay, we can drive out there and visit them. And if you're really nice, I bet we could even talk my cousin, Colton, into giving you a riding lesson. He's a pretty good teacher. He taught me how to ride."

Kajsa's eyes moved from the ground to Cassie. They had never looked so large or so blue. "You can ride?"

"I used to."

"And you really think he'd teach me?"

"I really do. But only if your dad says it's okay." Though Cassie couldn't imagine Noah not being okay with it.

"Can I come too?" Adelynn asked, apparently not liking the idea of being left out.

"You bet. You can even invite your dad if you want."

"I can't believe it!" Kajsa jumped out of her seat. Her entire body shook with excitement as she walked around the room, shaking her hands and jumping. "I want daddy to come right now so I can ask him."

Approximately fifteen minutes later—after Cassie had been bombarded with question after question about the ranch and the horses—Noah walked through the door, bringing a gust of chilly snow-filled air with him.

"I'm so sorry" was the first thing out of his mouth. "I tried to get out of there sooner, but—"

"Daddy, Daddy, guess what?" Kajsa barreled toward him and threw her arms around his waist. "Ms. Cassie's uncle owns a ranch with horses, and she says she can take all of us there and her cousin can teach me to ride a horse. His name's Colton. Isn't that a cool name? Can we go? Please? Please? Please?"

"Whoa, I'm not sure I caught all of that." Noah looked over his daughter's head at their dance teacher. "Is this true?" he mouthed.

She nodded.

His expression softened into one of tenderness before he crouched down in front of his daughter. "It looks like you're going to get the best early birthday present ever, princess."

"Does that mean we can go?" Kajsa asked.

"Of course it does."

Kajsa jumped up and down then threw her arms around her sister. "We get to ride a horse, Adi!"

"*You* get to ride a horse," Adelynn corrected. "I'm just going to watch."

"You can ride too, if you'd like to," said Cassie.

"No, I think I'll just watch."

They all laughed, then Kajsa grabbed her stuff and rushed toward the door. "I can't wait to tell Aunt Emma and Uncle Kevin and Aunt Becky and Sam! Maybe they can come too!"

"How about we just take a lot of pictures and show them later," said Noah.

In a swirl of snow and wind, Kajsa darted through the door, followed by Adelynn at a more sedate pace. Noah watched them go before taking Cassie by the shoulders and cocking his head. "You're full of surprises, aren't you?"

"How did your meeting go?" she asked.

His hands slid down her arms, then fell to his side. Noah shoved them in his pockets. The joy faded from his expression as he leaned against the wall. "They landed a big subdivision and want to hire me back."

"That's great news." She paused, watching him. "Isn't it?"

"They need me to start next week."

"Oh." Next week was spring break. Cassie knew because she'd had to cancel dance lessons for it. Noah had made plans with the girls—plans that would have to be unmade if Noah went back to work. "They can't wait another week?"

"It's next week, or they'll have to hire someone else."

"What are you going to do?"

"I don't know. I need the job, but it's really rotten timing. My sister and her husband have already planned a getaway trip for three of those days, and she invited Becky and her husband to come along. So besides having no one to watch the girls, it will also mean that your basement won't get finished on time either. I'm sorry." He smiled, but it didn't reach his eyes. He looked so tired and weighed down.

"I can take them," Cassie offered, surprised by how much she wanted to do just that, and not just to ease his burdens. Kajsa and Adelynn would be fun to have around for a few days.

Noah was shaking his head. "I would never ask you to do that. Please don't think that I brought it up to—"

"Why not? I'm not teaching next week, and my other work is so flexible that I can do it whenever."

"I thought you were planning to refinish your vanity next week."

She waved off his concern. "I can do that anytime.

136

Maybe we can even drop by the ranch one of the days so Kajsa can finally ride her horse." She paused. "Please let me help, Noah. I'd really love to have them around."

Noah watched her, as though trying to figure out if she was offering out of pity or because she really wanted to hang out with his girls. "Are you sure?" he finally said.

"I adore your girls. It's no problem at all. When do you need me to take them?"

"Wednesday through Friday."

"Perfect. I'll plan on it." That would give her Monday and Tuesday to work on the vanity and get some work done for Hansen Imaging.

Noah pushed away from the wall and interlocked his fingers with hers, pulling her close. His expression was one of gratitude and something stronger—something that made Cassie's heart hop, skip, jump, and freak out at the same time.

"I could kiss you right now," he murmured.

Mayday, mayday, mayday!

If she kissed him, there would be no going back. Only forward.

Cassie felt torn. She shouldn't want to kiss him, shouldn't be ready to kiss him, shouldn't be letting his hands frame her face. Everything was happening too fast.

Slow! she mentally yelled at her arms—arms that had somehow wormed their way around Noah's back. Traitors.

"Why are you hugging Ms. Cassie?" Adelynn's voice cut through the room.

Only then did Cassie feel the cold air swirling around them. She tried to pull free, but Noah's arms held her captive. He grinned down at her. "She's cold. I'm just warming her up."

"We're cold too," Adelynn complained. "It's *freeeezing* in the truck."

"All right, I'm coming." Noah loosened his hold, but his

eyes captured hers as he took a step back. "Rain check?" he said quietly.

No. No rain checks! Cassie tried to make her mouth form the words, but her head was already nodding. What was wrong with her?

Noah pressed a quick kiss against her cheek then walked out the door, allowing more cold air inside. But it wasn't until his taillights disappeared in the distance that the cold finally penetrated her body and she felt the need to pull on her sweatshirt. She hugged her arms tight against her chest, fearing and anticipating the day when he collected on that promise.

Sixteen

EXCITED VOICES CARRIED through the door of his daughters' room. Noah yawned and tried to rub the sleepiness from his eyes as he knocked on the door.

"You guys getting ready?" he asked needlessly. It was obvious they were.

"Yes!" they chorused, not sounding tired at all. The door opened, and Kajsa's youthful, radiant face smiled up at him. She wasn't normally a morning person.

"Can you put my hair in a ponytail today, Daddy?"

Noah blinked. He must be sleepier than he thought. He could have sworn Kajsa just asked him to—

"I want this brown elastic that will match my boots."

"Who are you, and what have you done with my daughter?"

She giggled and shoved the elastic in his face. "Please?"

His daughter was dressed in jeans, her favorite horse sweatshirt, and her one pair of cowboy boots. Noah had purchased them at Walmart, so they weren't exactly made for riding or tromping around on a ranch, but he wasn't about to tell her that. She looked adorable.

"It's going to cost you," he said.

"How much?"

"At least five hugs, five kisses, and five—"

Kajsa immediately wrapped her thin arms around her father's waist, giving him five quick squeezes. Then she stood on her tiptoes and pulled his shoulders toward her, giving him five rapid pecks on the cheek. "There. Now will you do my hair? I've got the vacuum all ready."

"And five tickles," Noah finished, tickling his daughter.

She squealed and giggled before finally wriggling free. Noah followed her into the room, where Adelynn was sitting in front of a mirror, brushing her hair out. "I don't have cowboy boots." She looked nervous. "Do you think they'll still let me come?"

"Just put on your old pair of sneakers, and you'll be fine." Not for the first time that week, Noah's chest tightened. It was killing him that he wouldn't get to see Kajsa's first official ride. Cassie had promised a ton of pictures and video footage, but it wouldn't be the same. Pictures were never the same. Noah wanted to be the one to swing Kajsa up on the horse for the very first time and be there to hug her when she came off. He wanted to see her ride and get caught up in the excitement right along with her.

Sometimes, being a grownup really stunk.

It didn't take too long to vacuum his girls' hair into ponytails and try to get them to eat at least one bowl of cereal. Then they were off, pulling into Cassie's driveway ten minutes later. As the girls scrambled from the truck, Noah lifted his face to the sun that was cresting the horizon. The crisp, April morning held the promise of a beautiful day.

They found Cassie's garage door halfway open, and vibrating sounds of a sander came from inside. Noah and the girls ducked under the door and saw Cassie down on her hands and knees, taking the varnish off the back of the vanity doors one swipe of the sander at a time. Her hair was coated in a fine sawdust, along with everything else in her garage, and dozens of crumpled sheets of wrinkled and beaten sandpaper were strewn around.

How long had she been at this?

Cassie glanced up and quickly turned off the sander. She brushed her jeans off and rose to her feet. "Wow, you're early," she said.

"Only by about fifteen minutes," said Noah. He'd wanted to arrive early so he could spend a little time with her before he had to take off for work. He didn't expect to find her covered in sawdust.

Her eyes widened. "Is it seven-thirty already?"

"Time flies when you're having fun, doesn't it?"

"Fun?" She glanced around at the mess she'd created. "No, this is not fun. It's the opposite of fun."

"You look old." Adelynn giggled.

"Well, I feel old." Cassie brushed her arms off. "My back aches, my hands have become sandpaper, and I swear I now have arthritis in my fingers—not that I know what arthritis feels like. Who in their right mind thinks this is fun? At the rate I'm going, it's going to take me an entire year to strip this stupid vanity down." She glanced at the girls. "If you're hungry, there are some muffins and juice on the counter just inside that door."

They both darted for the kitchen, leaving small footprints in the dust.

Cassie had obviously been hard at work the past couple of days. All the flat areas of the vanity had been completely stripped of stain and sanded down to the original wood. The intricate carvings still had a ways to go though. No wonder her fingers felt like sandpaper.

"I have no idea why I thought this would be a good idea." Cassie picked up a sanding block and tossed it into a box. "I've spent every spare second doing this since Monday and look how much more I still have to do? I'm beginning to hate this vanity as much as you do. There has got to be an easier way."

Noah bit his lower lip, wondering if it would be wise to tell her that yeah, there was a much—

"Wait, is there an easier way?"

He nodded slowly. "There's this cool product called stain stripper that will take the finish off a lot easier. All you'll have to do is brush it on, wait an hour or so, and scrape it off. I have some at home if you want me to bring it by later."

"Stain stripper?" She gaped at him. "Is there really such a thing?"

"I'm sorry, Cass. If I'd known you were going to completely strip it, I would have told you about it before now. But I thought you were going to paint it."

"I am," she said. Then her eyes grew wide with horror. "Oh my gosh. Please tell me that all this work hasn't been for nothing."

Noah hesitated. Of course he didn't want to tell her. But he didn't want her to do any more damage to her hands either. "Haven't you refinished wood before?"

"No. I watched a YouTube video on how to apply the antique stain, and they started with bare wood, so I figured I'd have to sand it all down."

Noah shouldn't laugh, but it was getting really hard to keep a straight face. Why hadn't she asked him for help? Why hadn't he made sure she knew what she was doing before she started? "Well, uh . . . you don't actually need to take off all the stain. A light sanding is all it needs. A good primer will cover up the rest."

Her expression took on an almost crazed quality. "You're really telling me the last two days have been a total waste?"

"Look on the bright side. At least you can stop sanding now. You've definitely done enough to make the primer stick."

She didn't look appeased.

"And think of the exfoliation benefits for your hands," he added.

"Noah!" she cried, clutching her head between her hands. "How could I have been so stupid?"

Unable to contain himself any longer, Noah chuckled. "Not stupid." he said, drawing her into a hug. "Definitely not stupid. You're just an over-achiever, that's all."

"Yeah, a stupid over-achiever. Oh my heck. I think I might cry."

Lips still twitching, Noah pulled her close and accidentally breathed in some of the sawdust from her hair. He sneezed, and Cassie's shoulders started to shake. He sneezed again, and a giggle escaped her mouth.

"Whew." He lifted his head and tried to brush the dust from her hair. "Let's get out of here. I think we can both use some muffins and juice, and I think the shower is calling your name."

"Don't you need to get to work?" she asked, allowing him to pull her inside.

"I can be a little late." He gave her a gentle shove toward her room. "Now shoo. Go shower so I can hug you without sneezing before I go."

She left a trail of dusty footprints down the hall, so Noah pulled out a broom and swept while Adi and Kajsa finished eating. When Cassie emerged ten minutes later with damp hair, it was time for him to go. He gave each of his girls a hug goodbye.

"Don't have too much fun without me," he said to them.

"Bye, Daddy," Kajsa said. "We'll take lots of pictures, I promise."

"You'd better."

Then he pulled Cassie close and kissed the top of her head. "Mmm, much better."

He was rewarded with a smile. "I'll see you tonight."

"Thanks, Cass. I really appreciate this."

"Anytime."

Noah left the house with a sense of loss. He liked his job, he did. Time flew by, and it kept him busy and involved in something he loved. But that didn't make it easy to leave behind his two little girls and a woman who entered his thoughts more often than not.

Seventeen

The crisp air was tainted with the smell of hay, manure, and earth. Cassie breathed in the once familiar scent, enjoying being back on the McCoy Ranch, where everything felt a little messy, a little cluttered, and a whole lot homey. Horses grazed in a corral off to the left, not far from the large, burnt orange barn where she used to play hide and seek. Off in the distance, a rooster cock-a-doodle-dooed and chickens clucked.

Man, she'd missed this place.

This used to be her getaway—her escape from reality. Cassie would drag her friends here, wanting them to experience this world where everything seemed simpler and more carefree. Her uncle would saddle up a horse or two and let them ride. Aunt Jane would fix them pumpkin cookies or marshmallow brownies. And her cousins would welcome them with big smiles and lots of teasing.

"Well, whaddayaknow. It's Cassie Ellis." Colton McCoy pulled her into a strong hug. "I didn't believe it when Mom said you were coming today. Aren't you a sight for sore eyes."

Cassie held him at arms' length so she could get a good look at him. "Holy cow, Colt. Look at you." He'd always been strong—working on a ranch had that effect on her cousins. But over the past two years, his awkward, gangly arms and shoulders had filled out, and those dark eyes looked older and wiser.

"You haven't changed a bit," he said.

"Well, you have." She tugged the brim of his cowboy hat down a notch. "Look how handsome you've become."

"That's what happens when you stay away." Colton pointed a finger at her. "People go and grow up on you."

"Yes, they do." Cassie had been wrong to cut herself off from everyone. She'd missed out on so much and denied herself the blessings of genuine, caring relationships, and for what? Nothing. Absolutely nothing. "You'd better get used to seeing me around here more often. I've missed you all too much to stay away any longer."

"Good to hear." He folded his arms and leaned against a wooden corral fence, looking beyond her. "I see you brought some troublemakers with you."

Cassie put her arms around the girls and scooted them closer. "Ladies, I'd like you to meet my favorite cousin, Colton McCoy. Colton, this is Adi and Kajsa."

"Howdy." He tipped his hat. "I hear you've come to ride some horses."

"She wants to," Adelynn corrected, pointing at Kajsa. "I'm just here to take pictures."

"That sounds boring," said Colton.

She screwed up her face. "Does it always smell yucky here?"

Chuckling, he pushed away from the fence and patted her head. "Don't worry, little lady. You'll get used to it." He led the way into the house, where Cassie and the girls were welcomed by sweet Aunt Jane's thin arms and a giant hug. Her straight, light brown hair was shorter now and bounced whenever she moved.

"Oh my goodness, it's so good to see you, you darlin' girl," Jane said. "How are you?"

"I'm good. Really good. Thanks so much for letting us drop by." Cassie introduced the girls, and Aunt Jane fed them some of her famous homemade oatmeal cookies and fresh milk. The girls devoured them, though Kajsa kept glancing out the back window toward the horse corral.

"What are their names?" she asked Colton, nodding in the direction of the horses.

He followed her gaze and smiled. "See that black horse on the far left?"

She nodded.

"That's Maverick. The light brown horse next to it is his girlfriend, Nutmeg. And then Whisper."

"Whisper?"

Colton bit off a large bite of cookie, chewed it a few times, then swallowed. "When we got him, he used to whinny so loud at night it kept us all awake. We figured if we named him Whisper, he'd take the hint and shut up."

Kajsa giggled. "Did he?"

As if on cue, Whisper lifted his head and let out a loud whinny.

"Nope," Colton said, staring out the window.

"I think you should have named him Trumpet."

That got a laugh out of Colton. "You're probably right." He pointed to the other side of the corral where a few more horses grazed. "Over there we've got Honey, Lancelot, and that little one we call Glitter."

It was Adelynn who giggled this time. "You named a horse Glitter?"

"Not really. Her real name is Cider. But not long after she was born, we found my little cousin leaning over the fence, giving her a shower of silver glitter. It took us forever to get her clean again, and even after all the washings, every once in a while, you could still catch a flash of glitter when the sun hit her just right. We started calling her Glitter after that, and the nickname stuck."

"Cider's a pretty name too," said Kajsa.

"I agree." He finished off his cookie. "I gave her that name."

Cassie watched the exchange from the corner of her eye, wishing Noah could be there to see Kajsa in her element. The smile hadn't left her face since they'd driven under the McCoy Ranch sign.

Colton pushed his chair back and stood. "Who's ready to ride some horses?"

"Me, me, me!" Kajsa was out of her seat before she'd said the last "me."

Adelynn eyed the beasts with a nervous expression. "Can I watch from the fence?"

"Sure," said Colton. "Just let me know if you change your mind and want to give it a try. Honey is the sweetest animal since . . . well, honey. And that's who we're going to saddle up for you gals today."

"Can I ride Maverick?" Kajsa asked as she bounded after him.

"I like your spirit, Kajsa." Colton patted her hair as they strode outside. "But no, Maverick is a horse for a little more advanced riders. Someday you'll be ready to ride her, but not today."

"Okay."

Cassie remained with Adelynn on the sidelines while Colton showed Kajsa how to catch Honey with her favorite treat—a carrot—and how to lead her to the barn and saddle her. The chestnut quarter horse was smaller in size and appeared sweet and docile—the perfect beginning mount. Adelynn snapped picture after picture, constantly calling out for Kajsa to smile or look her way. At first, Kajsa complied, but after a while, she finally glared at her sister.

"Can't you see I'm busy, Adi?"

"But Daddy says he wants lots of pictures."

"You've taken lots of pictures."

Cassie placed a hand on Adi's arm. "What about taking some candid shots now?"

"What's candid?"

"The informal kind, where Kajsa doesn't have to look and smile at the camera. You can take pictures of her profile or the natural expressions on her face when she first mounts the horse or the way she touches the animal without any fear. Candid shots can be some of the most beautiful pictures because they capture real emotion."

Adelynn slowly nodded. "Okay. I'll take some candid shots then."

"That's my girl."

Cassie leaned on the fence and watched as Colton taught Kajsa how to put one foot in the stirrup and hold on to the saddle. Then he gave her a small boost, and Kajsa was on the horse. The radiant smile that lit her face was something Cassie could only hope Adi had captured. Her sister had never looked more beautiful.

In no time at all, Kajsa went from being led around by Colton to walking and then trotting on her own. She was a natural.

Adelynn finally handed the camera back to Cassie with a sigh. "I'm getting bored," she said. "When can we go?"

Truth be told, Cassie was starting to get a little bored herself. But Kajsa didn't look like she'd be ready to quit anytime soon. "Are you sure you don't want to try riding Honey? She looks sweet."

Adelynn pursed her lips in thought then shook her head. "Maybe next time."

"Okay." Cassie held out her hand. "What do you say we see if Aunt Jane has any more of those yummy cookies?"

The little girl nodded, and together they walked back to the house. They found Aunt Jane setting out the makings for sub sandwiches for lunch. "I hope you're hungry," she said.

"Aunt Jane, you don't need to do this," said Cassie.

"Of course I do." She smiled. "It's not every day a favorite niece comes to visit, bringing two darling girls along. It'll be ready in a few minutes."

Adelynn glanced out the side window where a wooden swing hung from a giant maple tree. She pointed. "Can I go swing until it's ready?"

"Sure," said Cassie. "Do you need a push?"

"No, I can do it." She stole a cookie from the counter and was gone in a flash.

"What can I do to help?" Cassie asked. "And where's Uncle Mike and Dustin and Spencer?"

"They went to meet with someone about a mare that they're considering breeding with Maverick. They probably won't be back until tonight." Jane pointed to a pitcher on the counter. "Mind filling that up with ice water?"

"Happy to." As Cassie worked, she could feel her aunt's gaze on her. She glanced over her shoulder and caught her watching.

"They're adorable girls," Jane said. "Mind if I ask how you came to know them?"

"They're taking Irish dance lessons from me." She left it at that.

Jane gave her a knowing nod. "I talked to your mom this morning. She mentioned you're seeing someone. Are the girls any relation?"

Cassie laughed. "Are you sure she only 'mentioned' I was seeing someone?" After the grilling Cassie had gone through during the last Sunday dinner, her mother knew a lot more information than that. Tina hadn't exactly kept her run in with Cassie and Noah a secret.

Jane poured water into two glasses and handed one to Cassie before she eased her petite body into a seat at the table, gesturing for Cassie to do the same.

"I've missed you," said Jane. "We used to have such great talks, you and I."

"I know." Cassie looked at her glass, feeling the

melancholy that always came whenever she thought about what she'd given up for her so-called marriage.

"Your mom did fill me in a little more than I implied." Jane paused. "I'm sorry about what happened."

Cassie nodded, remembering the few times she'd brought Landon to the ranch. When they were dating, he'd been charming and outgoing and seemingly interested in the ranch. But it was all for show. Aunt Jane had seen right through him. She'd even tried to warn Cassie in her sweet and subtle way, but Cassie had refused to listen.

Condensation had collected on the outside of her glass, and Cassie used her thumb to swipe some of it away. "I should have listened to you," she said. "I shouldn't have rushed into things as fast as I did."

Aunt Jane's hand came to rest on hers. "Oh, honey. Love is blind. He was handsome, suave, and wealthy. What girl wouldn't be taken in by that?"

"You weren't." With the admission, something broke inside Cassie, and her eyes filled with tears. "How did I not see?"

Her aunt's hand squeezed hers. "It's in the past. He can't hurt you anymore."

"Oh, but he can," said Cassie. "I let him take me away from everything I loved, and I lost two years." Cassie gestured out the window. "I hardly recognized Colton. He looks so grown up, and I'm sure the younger boys will look even more so. I've missed out on two family rodeos, two mud football games, two Christmas parties, and a whole lot of talks. But what's worse, I think I've lost myself. And the thought of ever trusting someone else scares me to death."

Compassion appeared in Jane's eyes as she wiped one of Cassie's tears away. "Oh, darlin'. You don't see it, but you've gained so much too. You are older and wiser. You've learned things you probably don't realize you've learned yet. I see a wonderful maturity in you that wasn't there two and a half years ago, and that's not something you can dismiss. There's

151

a price that has to be paid for experience and knowledge, and sometimes it's a pretty steep price. But you've already paid it. So don't regret the past. Never regret the past. Value it. Use it. Be grateful for it."

The tears came more quickly now. How had Cassie gone two years without one of these talks, without the hope that her wonderful aunt always instilled in her? "Thank you, Aunt Jane." She sniffed.

"Now about the father of these girls," said Jane with a subtle smile. "Do you trust him?"

"I'm beginning to. We haven't been seeing each other very long, but he's wonderful. He really is."

"I'm looking forward to meeting him." Aunt Jane grabbed a box of tissues from the sofa table and passed it to Cassie, who blew her nose.

"Can I ask you a question?" Cassie said.

"Shoot."

"How long did you date Uncle Mike before you knew he was the one?"

Her aunt settled back in her seat, and a small smile played across her lips. "It took us a while. Two years, actually."

"Two years? Wow. That's a long time." At least for Cassie. Her entire marriage had lasted about that long, and it had felt like an eternity.

Aunt Jane smiled. "Our first kiss came six months after our first date. Your uncle—he moved as slow as molasses. But it was a good thing. By the time he finally got around to popping the question, I knew exactly what I'd be getting into, and I was prepared for it. We both were."

"And look at you now. Still happily married."

"Yes. Yes, we are." Aunt Jane leaned forward and gave Cassie's hand a squeeze. "Slow and steady wins the race, right? Especially when it comes to relationships."

"Exactly."

Her aunt was right. Cassie had learned the hard way that racing to the finish line wasn't the way to go. She and Noah needed to take their time and enjoy the journey. This go around, Cassie would be absolutely sure of the outcome before she ever said yes to anyone. And if it took two years to gain that confidence, then it would take two years.

When Noah's name appeared on Cassie's phone, her heart danced a little shuffle-hop-back. She placed her hand over her chest, willing it to calm down. After watching his girls for almost three days, Cassie should be used to hearing from Noah by now. He was constantly checking in with her, asking about the girls or telling her humorous things that had happened to him. And every time Noah's name accompanied the chime of a new text, her heart danced. Every time.

Completely ridiculous, not to mention stupid.

Cassie didn't want to be giddy. Giddy people did stupid things; they made rash decisions and eventually came to regret those decisions. Level-headed people, on the other hand, took their time, weighed out all the pros and cons, and made level-headed decisions.

That's who Cassie wanted to be. Not this giddy, heart-skipping girl whose judgment was so easily clouded by emotions. And yet, try as she might, she couldn't keep herself from reacting. Especially when Noah texted a question like,

Do you have plans tonight?

Cassie should have plans. She'd spent the past two days with the Mackie family. She had the girls during the day, and Noah joined them in the evenings. Last night, they'd played games, popped popcorn, and Noah hadn't left until nine.

She needed to take a break from them. From *him*. That's what rational, slow and steady people did. They took lots of breaks.

Who's asking? she finally answered. *A friend or a date?* If he said "date," she'd have plans. Lots of plans. Sorry-but-every-spare-minute-is-crammed-with-stuff-I-need-to-do plans.

Date, duh. Downgrading isn't an option, remember?

Cassie bit her lip. He was right. They couldn't exactly go back to being only friends. When it came to relationships, there was no going backward, only forward or nowhere at all. She would just have to make sure they took baby steps versus giant leaps.

No plans yet.

Want some?

Cassie hesitated only a moment. *Sure.*

Any chance you'd mind dropping by my house around 9:30?

His place? 9:30? After the girls were in bed? Cassie chewed harder on her lip. Great, now what? Why hadn't she just stuck with telling him about all her nonexistent plans?

Because she was a stupid, emotionally driven person. That's why.

Cassie was about to respond with a change of heart when another thought occurred. She needed to explain her slow and steady strategy to Noah. She needed to let him know that the rain check for the kiss couldn't be collected anytime soon. And she couldn't exactly do that with his daughters present.

So, it would actually be a good thing to meet up with him later. They could talk. Get on the same page. Become one with the page.

I'll be there, she finally wrote back.

Wear your dancing shoes. The soft ones. Not the hard ones with metal on the bottom.

Great. Now he wanted to dance? Cassie gave her lip a break and started chewing on her nail instead, feeling like she'd stumbled into some quicksand and was too far in to get herself out. They would just have to talk while they danced. Cassie could keep a level head while in his arms, couldn't she?

Oy vey. Yes, she was definitely deep in quicksand.

Another text chimed, and Cassie was almost afraid to look.

If you sing the wrong lyrics on any other songs, I want to know what they are.

But I don't know they're wrong until you start making fun of me.

TEASING, Cassie. Only teasing. CU soon.

Cassie's hand clamped over her dancing heart one more time. Then she took a deep breath and set her phone down. She needed to get her mind on other things before she had a panic attack.

"Girls, how do you feel about going grocery shopping with me?"

The expressions on their faces told Cassie they weren't thrilled by the prospect.

"I'll let you pick out a doughnut for dessert."

"Okay!" They dropped the markers they were using to color and went to find their shoes.

As Cassie watched them go, a melancholy feeling settled around her heart. Over the past few days, they'd had so much fun together. Besides the ranch, they'd crafted, shopped, danced, played, and cooked together. Cassie felt like she'd been given a taste of what it would be like to be a mother, and she liked how it tasted. A lot.

Too much.

It was a good thing that after today, she'd go back to being just their teacher. It wouldn't be wise for any of them to get used to being a family anytime soon.

Eighteen

THROUGH THE CURTAINS hanging across Noah's front window, Cassie could see the glow of what appeared to be little white lights framing the window. She hesitated on the front porch, pulling her jacket tighter around the long, flowing top she'd chosen to wear with her favorite charcoal leggings, thinking that she should have worn sweats instead.

What would happen if she knocked on the door and allowed herself to dance with Noah? What if he tried to kiss her? Would she be strong enough to say not yet? Two months ago, she only knew this man as the father of two little girls in one of her dance classes. Now she was about to spend the evening dancing with him.

A breeze whipped at her cheeks, and Cassie glanced at her car parked in the driveway. She should leave right now and send him a text that she'd changed her mind. He might be disappointed, but he'd understand.

Or—her gaze returned to the glowing window—she could knock and dance with Noah like they'd danced before.

No big deal.

Her mom used to tell her: "Don't run toward a relationship, but don't run away from it either. If it's right, it'll just happen."

It had sounded so easy, so smart. And Cassie had thought she was doing just that when she'd dated Landon. But looking back, she'd not only run toward marriage, she'd full on sprinted. She'd let the fog of twitterpation, fairy tales and romance cloud her judgment. Cassie hadn't really known Landon and he hadn't known her. It was like they'd fallen in love on a reality dating show, where nothing had been real. She'd been romanced, schmoozed, and swept off her feet. But she'd never been loved.

Looking back, it was all so clear to her now.

A shadow crossed in front of the window—a tall shadow with strong shoulders, a confident gait, and a good heart. Yes, it had only been two months since Cassie had met Noah. But in that short amount of time, he knew her better than Landon ever had—faults, quirks, Irish dancing, and all.

Maybe taking a small step forward wouldn't be such a bad thing.

Cassie lifted her hand and rapped on the door. A moment later, it opened, and the dark shadow became Noah. His face was freshly shaved, his hair was slightly damp, and he wore a fitted, button-down shirt that was as blue as his eyes. Her breath caught.

"Wow," said Noah. "You look beautiful."

"And you look . . . great." Too great. Her physical reaction to him was so strong that she wanted to sprint forward and forget all about taking her time.

Not good.

Noah opened the door wider. "Would you like to come in?"

Behind him, the soft glow of the lights created a sort of aura around him, and three beefy candles flickered on his bar. With the furniture pushed to the side, the room oozed romance. He probably smelled amazing too—just one more thing to sink her deeper into that quicksand.

Noah held out his hand. "Don't be nervous, Cass. It's just me."

That was the problem. Noah wasn't *just* anyone. He had the power to undo her. "Promise we won't move too fast." Her eyes pled with his.

"I promise," he answered, wiggling his fingers. "I loaded a lot of slow songs, so we'll be moving *very* slowly."

Her lips twitched as she rested her hand in his. "That's not what I meant, and you know it."

"I know. But a guy can tease, can't he? And your fingers are freezing." He closed the door and enclosed both of her hands in his, rubbing to try to warm them. "Does your car not have a heater?"

"It does. I just . . . Well, it took me a few minutes to work up the nerve to knock on the door."

"I'm glad you finally did. You would have turned into an ice sculpture if you'd stayed out there much longer."

She lifted her eyebrow. "It's spring in Colorado. Not winter in Antarctica."

"Does Antarctica even have a spring?"

"Probably a very cold one."

"Just like your fingers. How's the rest of you?" Noah tucked her arms around his back and drew her into a warm and cozy embrace. "Hmm . . . not nearly as cold, but not toasty either. I think you'd better stay here a while."

With her cheek pressed against his warm chest, Cassie's lips lifted. Just like she'd expected, he smelled good—like aftershave with a hint of soap. She breathed him in while her heart laced up its running shoes. And she didn't care at all. Instead, she snuggled closer and allowed his warmth to fill her up.

"Can I get you anything?" he asked.

"No." She wanted to stay right here. Just like this.

"What about ice cream? I've got cookie dough or mint

cookie dough. Maybe we could, you know, mix them together. I bet the combination would taste amazing."

Cassie looked up and shook her head. "You're incorrigible. You know that, right?"

"Maybe you should try to reform me."

"I don't think you're reformable."

"Yeah, you're probably right." His hands rubbed up and down her back. "So, I've been doing some thinking," he murmured into her hair.

"About what?"

"Your basement."

It was so unexpected that she pulled back with a laugh. "My what?"

He relinquished his hold around her waist and helped her to remove her jacket. Then he slung it over the arm of the couch and pressed a button on his mp3 player. Soft piano music crept into the room.

"Forget I said anything." Noah took her in his arms again, one hand resting at her waist, the other holding her hand. Even though he wasn't the most graceful dancer out there, the simple, old-fashioned hold took Cassie back to a different time, when men were raised to be gentlemen and women were treated with respect.

"I'm like an elephant. I never forget," she murmured. "So what about my basement?"

He spun her around, and her feet moved quickly and naturally to keep up. "You're a really good dancer." He was trying to change the subject.

"Noah," she said. "Out with it. What changes do you think I should make to my basement now?"

"None."

"Then why do you want to talk about it?"

"I don't."

"Yes, you do."

"Nope, I really don't."

Cassie pulled her hand from his, took a step back, and

folded her arms. "I refuse to dance until you tell me what it is."

He shoved his hands in his pockets and glanced at his feet. "Okay. Here goes. How would you feel about me contracting out the rest of the work?"

The smile on Cassie's face wanted to fall, but she forced it to stay put.

It was a silly reaction. Someday, her basement would be finished, and Noah wouldn't show up to saw or bang or sand or play his music too loud. At first those sounds had annoyed her, but over the past several weeks, she'd come to look forward to them. There was a reason she no longer worked on choreography while he was at her house, and it wasn't because he hated Irish music. It was because she liked to hear him work. After he was gone, she liked to go down there and see the results of his work. Noah had become her favorite part of her basement. He was in every nail, every wall, and every light. The thought of him not being in the rest of it—the finishing touches—left Cassie feeling achy inside.

Yet at the same time, she understood why he wanted to let someone else do the rest of the work.

"It's because of Adi and Kajsa, isn't it? You don't want to leave them in the evenings."

Worry filled Noah's expressive brown eyes. She knew he didn't want to disappoint her, but at the same time, his girls came first. As they should. It was one of the many things she admired about him.

"I'm sorry," he said. "I hate the thought of having to pass the rest of the project off to someone else, but I'm already relying on Becky and Emma to be there for them the few hours after school that I can't be there. I can't be gone all night too."

"You can bring them to my house," Cassie blurted without thinking. So much for being level headed and not getting used to being a family anytime soon. None of that seemed to matter anymore. "We can eat dinner together, like we have been, and then you can work for a few hours while I hang out with the girls upstairs. They can come down and talk to you whenever they want, or you can come up and—"

"Cassie, I'm not going to let you do that."

"But I *want* to." She moved forward and placed her hands on his arms. "Really, Noah, I do. I've had so much fun with them the past few days, and I would love to spend more time with them. But I'll also understand if you still want to hire it out. I know how important they are to you."

He shook his head and started to open his mouth—probably to disagree—but Cassie pressed her fingers against his lips to keep him quiet. "Just think about it, okay?"

"Okay," he said. His breath was warm and his lips soft. Cassie melted.

Without thinking, she let her thumb travel the length of his lower lip. What would it feel like to kiss him? What would he taste like? How would he respond?

Why was she even thinking about this?

The screeching sound of bagpipes blared through the speakers, saving Cassie from doing something impulsive. From the disgruntled look on Noah's face, he didn't agree.

She had to laugh. "What is this?"

"You, of all people, should know that. It's Irish music."

"There are no bagpipes in Irish music."

"Well, this was the closest I could find."

Were they supposed to dance to this? Cassie almost laughed again. "You hate this kind of music. Why are we listening to it?"

"Because I want you to teach me some of your fancy moves."

Cassie laughed again. "Are you serious?"

"Deadly."

She shook her head, still smiling. "Okay, but don't forget you asked for it."

"I won't."

Cassie tried to teach him the simplest of dances—the light jig. But when it came to kicking and skipping and quick little steps, he couldn't get the hang of it. After several attempts, he finally gave up and started performing a hilarious form of Russian dancing, where he squatted and attempted to kick his legs out while folding his arms. Cassie laughed so hard she had to clutch her stomach.

"Just to See You Smile" by Tim McGraw came on next, and Noah pulled Cassie close. He rocked her back and forth with exaggerated movements, taking quick steps backwards.

"Is this supposed to be the two-step?" She was fighting not to smile.

"Am I doing it wrong?"

"Where did you learn how to do it?"

"A YouTube video."

Cassie's cheeks were beginning to hurt from smiling so much. She slowed him to a stop. "Let's try this. Put your weight on your right foot," she coached. "Then, starting with your left, move your feet in a quick-quick, slow, slow pattern. Like this." She demonstrated, counting, "One-two, three, four. One-two, three, four."

Noah repeated the numbers under his breath, and after a minute or so, he finally got it. Sort of. His quick steps were a tad too fast and his slow a tad too slow. And when he tried to dance around the room again, his footwork became confused, and he ended up doing more of a quick, slow, slow, quick-quick pattern—not that he ever repeated the same steps. The song ended with him trying to spin Cassie the way the "professionals" had done it in the video.

After the two-step, they swing danced to Billy Joel, cha-chaed to Jennifer Lopez, and waltzed to Enya. At some point, Cassie gave up trying to teach him the correct moves and instead attempted to match her footwork to his as best she could. They ad-libbed a seventies dance to Abba and hip hopped to Black Eyed Peas. Noah spun her around until she got dizzy, stepped on her toes a few times, and dipped her at the end of every dance.

Cassie couldn't remember ever having so much fun.

And then "Amazed" by Lonestar came on. Breathing hard from the hip hop moves, Noah fisted an imaginary microphone and mimicked a DJ's deep voice. "All right, people, we're going to slow things down now. So guys, ask that beautiful girl you've had your eye on all night to dance, and girls, do him a favor and say yes. This one's for you."

The pretend microphone dropped to his side, and Noah held out his hand. "Cassie Ellis, would you like to dance with me?"

Could this man get any more adorable? She placed her hand in his and stepped into his arms. She melted into him and rested her head in the hollow of his chest.

"Is Irish music the only kind you don't like?" she murmured.

"As long as you're dancing to it, I love Irish music."

"What about bluegrass? Are you a fan of that?"

"For the most part."

She looked up at him. "Jazz?"

"It's okay."

"African?"

"Yes."

"Rap?"

"Not my favorite, though there are a few cool songs out there."

"Opera?"

He made a face. "Not so much. Why all the questions?"

"Where you use ice cream to figure out people, I use music." Cassie didn't really, but his extensive tastes intrigued her. Noah liked pretty much everything, or at least a taste of everything. Was he as accepting with people? Would he care if the colors she wore clashed with her hair? Would it bother him if she left her hair down for a fancy company party? Would he tell her she was too old to keep her favorite stuffed animal on her bed? Get annoyed if he found something out of place?

No. He wouldn't care about any of that. Noah shoved ice cream in freezers, wore jeans with holes in them, and danced with two left feet.

Noah was real.

He was genuine.

And he was frowning at her.

"I'm not sure I want you to use music to psychoanalyze me," he said. "The fact that I'm not a fan of that Irish stuff yet love hard rock can't be good in your eyes."

She smiled up at him. "Don't worry. You already passed with flying colors."

"Really?" The tips of his lips lifted into a small smile, like he was mentally giving himself a pat on the back. "Are you going to tell me the criteria you used to judge?"

"Nope."

He chuckled, and his chest vibrated. Cassie felt an overpowering sensation of being sucked in and held captive. Was this what it felt like to be bewitched by someone? Her gaze moved from his eyes to his lips.

Kiss me came the involuntary thought.

Ever so slowly, Noah cupped the back of her head and lowered his mouth to hers. At first, his lips moved cautiously, feeling, touching, and sampling, and then his hands moved to the sides of her face, and the kiss increased in intensity. Cassie was pulled into a beautiful, starlit world where no pain or heartbreak existed. Only peace and joy and wonder. In this world, it was easy to forget all about slow and steady and believe that happily ever afters weren't just in fairy tales.

Cassie's arms wound around his back, and her fingers pressed into his shirt. Noah was different than Landon. He was wonderful and mesmerizing and amazing and wow, could he kiss. Cassie felt herself falling, falling, falling. She envisioned making a life with Noah. Pictured raising his daughters as hers. Dreamed of walking down the aisle in a beautiful white dress and saying yes, yes, yes.

Alarms sounded in her head. *Yes? Yes? Yes?* Was she insane? What was she thinking? Cassie wasn't Cinderella, this room wasn't a castle, and Noah wasn't a prince. People didn't fall madly in love in two months, glass slippers didn't exist, and fairy tale endings didn't just happen because you wanted them to. Had she learned nothing from Landon?

Cassie pressed her palms against Noah's chest and broke free.

"You can't"—dang, she was out of breath—"kiss me like that. Not yet."

"Why?" Beneath her palms, his chest rose and fell as rapidly as hers.

"Maybe in six months, but not now."

"Six months?" Noah laughed as though she'd made a joke, then stopped when he saw she wasn't joining in. "Wait, are you serious?"

"You promised we'd go slow, Noah. This isn't slow."

His fingers curled around her upper arms, and his eyes met hers. "Cassie, it was just a kiss. Just. A. Kiss."

Maybe for him. For her, it was an Olympic-paced one-hundred yard dash.

"When two people are dating, it's normal to kiss."

She pulled free and pointed at him. "Yes, but not like that. That kiss was not . . . normal." It was a spell he'd cast on her, making all common sense go bye bye.

His lips twitched. "Then what was it, exactly?"

"Not normal!" Good grief. Why was he giving her a hard time about this? Why wasn't he reeling and as freaked out as she was?

"Well, I'm a fan of the abnormal then, because I thought it was amazing." He took a step closer. "In fact, I'd really like to repeat—"

"No! Not for six more months!" She held up her hand to stop him from coming any closer. "At least!"

"You said that already." He continued to inch forward.

"I mean it." Cassie's back hit the door, and a feeling of claustrophobia overtook her. She couldn't keep resisting him. She needed distance. She needed fresh, unromantic air. She needed her aunt to douse her with a large pitcher of ice water. And she needed Noah to understand.

His footsteps stilled, his expression softened, and the teasing glint left his eyes. "I was only teasing, Cass. If you really think we're moving too fast then we'll slow down. But six months is a bit extreme, don't you think?"

She shook her head, trying to convince herself as much as him.

Noah sighed and nodded, then took a step back. "Okay. Six months it is. But if you change your mind feel free to let me know." He gave her a small smile as he picked up her coat and helped her put it on. "I wish I could drive you home. It's late."

"I'll be fine."

"Will you let me know when you arrive?"

"Yes."

His eyes captured hers in a look that seemed to say, "Be brave and don't freak out." But when it came to moving forward, Cassie didn't want to be brave. She wanted to be strong and set. She wanted to be absolutely sure. And as much as she wanted to believe that happily ever afters did exist, two months wasn't enough time to know anything.

Rising to her tiptoes, Cassie placed a soft kiss on his cheek. "Thank you for the dances. You made me feel like a lady tonight."

His hand caught hers before she could step away again. "You are a lady, Cass, and I'll always treat you that way. Never forget that."

She felt herself falling under his spell again, so she pulled her hand free. Then she opened the door and fled into the night, feeling like Cinderella at the stroke of midnight.

Only tomorrow, there would be no glass slipper, no impromptu proposal, and no rushing into any of it.

She wasn't Cinderella and didn't want to be.

Nineteen

THE AIR SMELLED like earth and vegetation and spring. The buds on the trees were beginning to uncurl into green leaves, and the snow from the previous weeks' storm had all but disappeared. It was a time of year that Noah both loved and dreaded. The promise of warmer weather, his girls riding bikes or running through sprinklers, outdoor barbeques, and late night talks on the porch with Emma, Kevin, Becky, and Justin. He looked forward to it all. But at the same time, the girls would be out of school during the time when the construction industry was at its peak. So in that respect, summer was the most difficult time of year for him.

"C'mon, you stupid thing. Come out!" Across the street, Becky tugged with all her might on a large weed that had sprung up in the middle of one of her budding shrubs. Her yard was always pristine. It was a normal thing to see her weeding or planting or trimming. But she didn't normally yell at the weeds, and she never wore slacks and a dress shirt. Something was wrong.

Noah eyed Emma's house with longing, wanting to see his girls and feel their hugs around his neck. But Justin was out of town for the week, which meant Becky was dealing with whatever it was all alone. So he crossed the street just in time to hear Becky cuss. Becky never cussed.

For a brief moment, Noah wondered if he should let her cool off a little before he tried to get to the bottom of things. Maybe it would be better to give Justin or Sam a call. Or there was always Emma. Women seemed to be so much better at consoling other women. Yes, he should go get Emma.

He was about to turn around when Becky's hands slipped from the weed, and she fell back on the ground. Her head dropped to her knees, and quiet sobs shook her body. Noah's eyes widened. Becky never cried either. Oh geez. Had something happened to Justin or Sam?

He rushed forward and knelt beside her, putting an arm around her shoulders. "Becky, what's wrong?"

She sniffed and glanced up at him, then ran the back of her hand across her eyes, leaving traces of mud across her cheeks. "I can't"—she drew in a shuddering breath again—"get that stupid"—another breath—"weed out."

Noah gave her arm a gentle squeeze. "Here, let me." With one hard yank, he pulled the roots free, sending dirt clods flying. One hit Becky on the forehead, and she half cried, half laughed.

"I'm sorry," said Noah, using his sleeve to wipe it off.

"No, it's okay." She sniffed again. "I actually needed that."

Noah took in her muddy knees and dirt splattered shirt. "Is everything okay with Sam and Justin?"

She waved away his concern. "They're fine. More than fine, actually. And I'm fine too. Really. I'm just"—she wiped her eyes and sniffed   again—"being stupid, that's all. Don't mind me. Go home and be with your girls."

Her appearance belied her words. Besides the mud, her

eyes and nose were a miserable shade of red. He wasn't about to leave her like this.

Noah sank down on the grass across from her and rested his arms around his knees. "You're crying, and you just swore, Becky. I hate to break it to you, but you're not fine. So what's up?"

Another shuddering breath, and Becky stared at the horizon. "Sam accepted a summer internship in South Carolina." She uttered another half cry, half laugh. "See? This is great news, right? There were hundreds of applicants, and *she* got the job because she's talented and vivacious and wonderful. This is definitely not something to cry about."

Noah suddenly felt like cursing and crying himself. The thought of an entire summer without Sam was a depressing one. They wouldn't hear her laughter fill the quiet streets, wouldn't be forced to have a water balloon fight (which they all secretly loved), wouldn't see her amazing sidewalk chalk sketches or taste the chocolate chip cookies that only Sam could get just right. And besides that, who would step in as his daughters' favorite nanny for the summer?

Adi and Kajsa were going to be devastated.

Noah plucked a blade of cold grass and twirled it between his fingers. "I'm sorry, Beck. We're all going to miss her."

"She says she has a really good friend who would make a great nanny. You know, if you still need one this summer."

Noah nodded. "I might have to take her up on that."

"It's only for a few months, and she'll be back here for school. This is just temporary, right? If the company offers her a permanent job after she graduates, it's not like she'd accept. I mean . . . she wouldn't, would she?" Becky's red-rimmed eyes turned to him, pleading for him to agree.

"No, she wouldn't," Noah said automatically, even though he didn't necessarily believe it. Sam was young and talented and smart. If an amazing opportunity landed in her lap, he'd want her to snatch it up no matter where it took her. And Becky would too.

Becky glanced back at the ground, and another tear fell. "Everything is going to change, isn't it? Sam will grow up and leave for good, you'll marry Cassie and move to her house, and Emma and Kevin will eventually find something bigger and nicer. Meanwhile, Justin and I will be here alone, with him on the road half of the time."

Noah leaned forward and gave her knee a squeeze. "You're right. Some things will change. But no matter where any of us go, we'll always be family. And Sam will always be your daughter. We'll never stop getting together, and she'll never stop coming home. That, I promise you, won't change."

"I know, but—" Becky shot him a sideways look. "Wait. You didn't instantly deny the whole marrying Cassie thing. Does that mean you're thinking about it?"

Noah had no one but himself to blame for that. He leaned back on the grass and sighed. "It means I'd marry her tomorrow if she'd let me. But she's scared, and I'm not sure when—and if—she'll ever stop being afraid." A glow over the horizon captured Noah's attention, and he stared at a sky that had become a wonderland of pinks, oranges, blues, and purple. He couldn't remember the last time he'd seen such a striking sunset.

"She'll come around," said Becky with confidence. "I just hope it's sooner than later. If there's anything Sam has taught me, it's that life passes by way too quickly to ever waste a second."

Noah considered her words as the sun sank lower in the sky and the colors began to fade. Another reminder that most things didn't last forever. Would Cassie be one of those things?

He tossed aside the mashed blade of grass and jumped up. "C'mon. Let's go to Emma's and get some dinner. I think we could both use hugs from Adi and Kajsa."

"Agreed," Becky said, this time able to smile without

sniffing. "But Justin should be finished with his meetings by now, so I think I'm going to go change and give him a call first—if Sam hasn't already beaten me to it. She's so excited."

"As she should be."

"I know."

Noah nodded. "Don't be long. I'll have the girls help me make some sort of celebratory dessert. How's that?"

"It sounds wonderful." She stood and began dusting off her pants.

"And Becky?"

"Yeah?"

"Everything is going to be okay. You'll see."

She nodded and gave him a half smile. "Thanks, Noah."

Glancing at the sky one last time, Noah strode forward, more determined than ever to not let Cassie slip away.

The little white lights wrapped around his daughters' headboards cast a soft glow around the room. The girls plugged them in every night and occasionally remembered to unplug them in the morning.

Noah lay at the foot of Adi's bed, listening to them breathe. Adi's sleep was quiet and gentle, whereas Kajsa flipped from one side to the other, tangling her covers between her legs. As a little girl, she used to fall out of bed at least once a week, and eventually, Adi had demanded they get separate beds. She was tired of getting kicked awake throughout the night.

It always amazed Noah how two girls from the same parents could be so different from each other and yet individually special at the same time. Even more amazing was the fact that Cassie seemed to see the same thing. She and Adi shared the bond of Irish dance and all things girly, but Cassie had also been able to form a strong connection with Kajsa as well. Both of his girls couldn't stop talking about the three days they'd spent with her. When could they hang out with her again? When, when, when?

Noah didn't know what to tell them. After the "not normal" kiss they'd shared, he'd kept his distance, hoping she'd come to her senses and realize that kiss had been "not normal" because it had been perfect. The thought of waiting six months to feel her lips against his, her fingers in his hair, or the way her body melted against his—now *that* was not normal.

Noah could barely handle the five days they'd spent apart. Five. Long. Missing-Cassie-like-crazy days. They'd exchanged a few texts here and there, but that was it. And it wasn't enough.

Life passes way too quickly to ever miss a second.

Becky's words thudded inside his brain. Wasn't that what he and Cassie were doing right now? Wasting seconds? *A lot* of seconds? The past five wasteful days could have been spent hanging out, laughing, seizing the moment, and perfecting that already perfect kiss.

It was time to end this craziness.

Noah sat up and tiptoed from the room. The moment he'd closed his bedroom door, his phone was out of his pocket, and he was calling Cassie.

Pick up. Please, pick up.

"You're calling late," she finally answered.

"Five days is way too long to go without seeing you."

Silence. Followed by, "Actually, it's only been four days and twenty-three hours."

"I rounded up."

"I noticed."

"Cassie . . ." Noah didn't know how to finish the sentence. *Will you just marry me?* wouldn't exactly go over well.

"I miss you too," she finally said.

Enough to come over right now and dance with me

again? Enough to admit that we aren't moving too fast? And that six months was a ridiculous amount of time to go without kissing? It was simple physics. An object (or two, in this instance) in motion will stay in motion unless acted upon by an unbalanced force. Cassie needed to stop being that unbalanced force. Motion was natural. Moving forward was natural. Stopping abruptly or being thrown off course—not so much.

Noah sat on his bed and leaned forward, resting his forehead on the palm of his hand.

"Noah? You still there?"

"Yeah. I've just been doing some thinking."

"About my basement again?" she said dryly. He could hear the smile in her voice.

Noah had definitely missed her. She'd become a major ingredient in the recipe for his happiness, and the past five days had been way too bland. "No. I mean, yes. Well, sort of. I've actually been thinking about your offer to watch the girls while I finished your basement, and I'm wondering if the offer is still good."

A slight hesitation on her end, and then, "Yes. It's still good. When would you like me to start?"

"Would tomorrow be too soon?" Noah held his breath.

Another pause. "Tomorrow's perfect. I'll bring them home from dance with me, and you can meet us at my house."

A feeling of relief washed over Noah, and he flopped back on the bed. "Great. It's a date then."

"Is it?" Her voice was still smiling.

"Yes. I thought we already came to an agreement on this. Once a date, always a date. Unless, of course you want to upgrade me to—"

"It's a date."

"Great."

"Yes, great."

The silence that followed made Noah smile. Apparently

Cassie didn't want to end the call anymore than he did.

"You're not going to believe what happened to Adi today."

"Tell me."

And Noah did. He told her about the Irish dance solo Adi was asked to perform during her school play. Then he told her about Kajsa and how she'd checked out every book in the library on the subjects of barrel racing and rodeos and how she wanted a cowboy hat just like Colton's. And then he told her about the frustrating homeowner he'd been working with—or at least *trying* to work with.

"I think Spencer hired me back just so he could pass this woman off to me. She's a nightmare, I tell you. Every time I talk to her, she has changed her mind about something. We poured her foundation for her house over the weekend, and today she shows up holding a new floor plan with the front porch and garage flip-flopped and the kitchen in a different location."

"Are you kidding me?"

"No. She realized that the front porch would get the full brunt of the afternoon sun and didn't want that. I told her to just plant a tree, but she didn't like that idea. She wants the porch on the other side of the house."

"Oh no. Does she have a basement? Are you going to have to excavate and backfill that too?"

"No, thank heavens. That's the only positive to the story."

They continued to talk for another hour before Noah's yawn had him glancing at the clock. "I should let you go."

"Yeah. It is getting late. I'll see you tomorrow."

"K. Oh, and Cass?"

"Yes?"

"Thanks."

"No problem."

The following day, Noah drove straight to Cassie's house after work. He was greeted with two little bear hugs, along with tantalizing smells coming from the kitchen. He kept one eye on Cassie as she finished dinner preparations while his girls interrupted each other, telling him about their days. It felt a little surreal, like this was really his house and his family—a day in the life of what could be.

It felt good.

"I hope you like crock pot meals," said Cassie after the girls had returned to their homework. "Now that spring break is over and dance lessons are back in session, I didn't have much time to get dinner ready."

Noah completely understood. "I'll eat anything, and that smells amazing. But you don't have to cook for us. We can either come over after dinner, or we can bring dinner to you half the time."

She waved him off. "I don't mind having dinner ready. It's actually nice to cook for more than just me. Besides that, you've got a whole night of work waiting for you, whereas I get to play and hang out with Adi and Kajsa."

Noah moved to her side and lifted the lid of the crock pot. What looked like gooey lasagna cooked inside, smelling so good he wanted to grab a fork and take a bite. He replaced the lid and pulled Cassie into his arms. "You're pretty amazing," he murmured.

She smiled. "My mom always told me that a way to a man's heart is through his stomach. I guess she was right."

"No," he said. "If that was a Marie Calendar freezer meal, I'd still think you're amazing. What can I do to help?"

"Set the table?"

"Done."

"Daddy, I don't get this." Kajsa was frowning at the few pages of homework she was working on.

Noah grabbed a stack of plates from the cupboard and went to her side, helping her work through a math problem while he set the table. Then he tested Adi on her spelling words.

After dinner, he helped rinse the dishes despite Cassie's protests. Then she turned on a movie for the girls while she helped him haul the interior doors and frames inside.

"I have a favor to ask you," Noah said as they maneuvered their way down the basement stairs.

"Another one?" Cassie teased. "Noah, you ask too much."

"I know, I know. But this won't be hard. I promise." Noah set his end of the door down and took the other side from Cassie, tilting it up against the wall. He turned to find her watching him expectantly.

"Well?" she said.

Noah brushed his hands off. "Actually, it's more of a promise. From now until I'm finished with your basement, I want you to give me your word that you won't come down here."

She blinked at him, her eyes wide. "You call that easy? Because it's not. I like coming down here to check out all your progress. I want to see the floors after they go in. I want to see if the paint colors I chose will look good. I want to see what the vanity looks like in the bathroom. And I want to see—"

"Me?" Noah interrupted, unable to resist teasing her.

"No. I mean of course. But that's not what I was going to say."

"Ouch, Cass. That hurts."

She playfully slapped his arm. "Stop teasing me for once and don't ask me not to come down here."

"Please?" Noah cocked his head to the side, pleading with her.

"Why?"

He smiled. "Because I want to see your face when you see it all done. Not partly done, but all."

She stepped into him, encircling his waist with her arms. "But you'll get to see my face a lot more if you let me

178

come down here every day. And don't you dare say you don't want to see my face, because I know you do."

He chuckled. "You're right. But in this situation, I'd really love for you to wait."

She scratched at a splatter of paint on his chest. "The things you ask of me."

"Will you promise?"

She sighed. "Okay. I promise."

Noah thanked her with a kiss on the cheek. "That's legal, right?"

Cassie smiled and stepped from his arms. "I should go check on Adi and Kajsa."

"And I should get to work on these doors."

"I guess I'll see you when I see you then." She offered him a parting wave.

Noah's gaze lingered on the graceful sway of her hips as she trotted up the stairs, and the moment she disappeared from sight, he got to work.

It was time to make this basement look like a home.

Snuggled between Adelynn and Kajsa, Cassie watched the movie *Tinker Bell and the Great Fairy Rescue* with her thoughts hovering somewhere between reality and Neverland, where kids stayed young forever, and adult worries didn't exist. *Peter Pan* had been one of her favorites as a child, and when *Hook* came out, she'd loved that too. Up until Landon, her life had been so full of happy memories that if Tinker Bell had sprinkled pixie dust on her, Cassie would have soared.

Too bad she'd had to grow up and get some not-so-great memories. She couldn't fly with those.

You don't have any not-so-great memories with Noah.

It was a good thought, a hopeful thought, and one

Cassie clung to. So far, the memories Noah had given her were happy, wonderful ones—the kind that could easily send her gliding through the skies. Why did she feel the need to stall? She should be running forward, making more and more good memories so there would be no more room for the not-so-good ones.

"That would be so cool," Kajsa said to no one in particular. She was staring at the movie.

Pulled from her thoughts, Cassie refocused on the screen and saw the little girl that Tinker Bell had befriended fly.

Peter Pan's words came to mind.

With a little faith, trust, and pixie dust, anything is possible.

Maybe it was time to stop holding back. To put her faith and trust in Noah and see what came of it. Her Aunt Jane had been right. Cassie was older and wiser now. She'd learned how to discern between a good guy and a not-so-good guy, and Noah was good. She could feel it.

By the time the movie ended, both girls had fallen asleep. Kajsa had moved to the floor and was sprawled across the large woolen area rug whereas Adelynn had snuggled into Cassie's lap. While the credits rolled, Cassie combed her fingers through Adelynn's soft curls.

She looked down, and a tenderness she didn't expect swelled inside her. Adi was smart, kind, and determined. She had a natural grace and flexibility that would turn her into a beautiful dancer one day if she kept at it. And Kajsa's adventurous side would lead her to some fun and exciting places. Cassie wanted to be part of both girls' journey. To see them grow and mature. Be there for them when they fell down or experienced heartbreak, as they one day would. She wanted to see their smiles, hear their laughter, cheer them on, and be someone they turned to when life got hard.

Was this what it felt like to be a mom?

It was an overwhelming emotion, and one Cassie had

never experienced before. She blinked and realized her eyes were wet with tears.

"Everything okay?" Noah's quiet voice made her jump and quickly wipe her eyes.

Adelynn stirred and moaned, and Cassie carefully slid sideways, replacing her lap with a throw pillow. She turned off the TV before facing Noah, hoping that he hadn't noticed the tears.

He pulled her against him and smoothed his hands up and down her back. He smelled like sawdust and felt like heaven.

"What's wrong?" he said.

"Nothing." And she meant it. Absolutely nothing was wrong. Everything had never felt more right.

"Get much done?" she asked.

His focus returned to her. "The frames are all hung, along with the trim in the family room. I'll start painting tomorrow.

"Paint? Already?" It would be so difficult not to take a peek downstairs when paint fumes replaced sawdust. Her basement was finally coming together, and she couldn't see it until it was all done.

"If all goes well, I should be done in a couple more weeks."

A smile stretched across her face. "I finished the vanity over the weekend."

"Can I see it?"

"Only if you promise to not call it kitschy or gaudy or any other synonym."

He smiled. "I'll try to keep my opinions to myself this time."

"Good."

He followed her out to the cool garage, and she flipped on the light. All evidence of sawdust, sandpaper, or paint cans had been removed, and all that was left was a newly painted antiqued vanity. Cassie watched his expression as he examined it.

"You did a good job on the paint," he finally said.

She laughed at his attempt to say something positive and stepped next to him. "I hate it."

"What?" His head swung around to face her.

"I said I hate it." Every time Cassie walked into the garage, she liked it less and less. But she'd still painted it, still glazed it, and still lacquered it. It was like she'd wanted to prove that she could turn the ugly duckling into a swan of a vanity.

It hadn't worked.

"Since when?"

"Since I realized you were right about Landon never seeing it and me having to live with it." She shook her head. "I should have listened to you."

"What are you going to do with it?"

She shrugged. "For now? Keep it. We've already ordered the sink and counter, and it's painted and ready to go. Someday, I'll replace it with something else—maybe something we both like."

Noah watched her closely. One at a time, he picked up her hands, interlocking them with his. "Does my opinion really matter?"

Cassie drew in a deep breath. "Yes."

His gaze traveled from her eyes to her lips, and Cassie's heart sped up. She lifted her face to his, and he met her halfway, stopping inches from her face. The warmth of his breath teased her senses.

"Do I still have to wait six months to kiss you again?" he murmured. "Because I really, *really* want to kiss you right now."

"Did I say six months?" Cassie said. "Because I meant six days."

"I'm in luck then. It's been six days."

"No, it has only been five days and twenty-two hours."

"But I've already warned you. I round up." Not giving her a chance to argue, his lips pressed firmly against hers. There was no hesitancy, no easing his way into the kiss this time. He was just there, crushing her against him with a confidence she envied. How could he be so sure about her? Where were his doubts, his worries, his hang-ups? Where?

Cassie didn't want to wait two years for that confidence to come. She wanted it now. So she kissed him back and she kissed him hard, yearning for the same assurance that seemed to come so easy to him.

Maybe if she let him carry her for a while, it would.

Twenty

THREE WEEKS HAD never passed so fast. As April became May and the days grew longer and warmer, Cassie found herself spending nearly every day with the Mackie family. Noah would work four nights a week on her basement, reserving Wednesdays and weekends for his girls and Cassie. They went hiking and biking. They'd picnicked in the park, dropped by a local petting zoo to feed the animals, had dinner with Emma and Kevin, and rode horses at the McCoy's ranch. They'd eaten together, worked together, and played together.

Cassie found that their relationship settled into a slow and steady pattern. He kissed her every chance he got, but that was okay. They were getting to know each other, trying on what it would feel like to be an actual family, and exploring what could be. They were dating. Taking their time dating.

Cassie looked forward to every single evening with the Mackies.

"Look, Adi, Aunt Becky's here!" Kajsa's voice called from the foyer.

From inside the studio, Cassie glanced through the open door to see Becky giving the girls hugs.

"Guess what?" Becky said to them. "Instead of going home with Cassie, you get to come with me. I have pizza in the car and a movie waiting for you at home. Who's excited? I know I am. It's been way too long since I've gotten to spend time with my two favorite girls."

"Is it a horse movie?" Kajsa asked, moving from her heels to her toes the way she always did when excited.

"It's a surprise."

Cassie slipped past a few students and walked into the foyer to meet them. "Becky, hey. What's up?"

"Girls, run and change your shoes while I talk to Cassie for a sec, okay?"

The girls complied, and Becky smiled. "I'm giving you the night off," she said. "Actually, Noah's giving you the night off."

But Cassie didn't want the night off.

"Something came up at his work, so he asked me to pick up the girls tonight. Didn't he tell you?"

"He probably texted, but I've been in class." Cassie had planned to make his favorite dinner tonight. The salmon was marinating in her fridge, the fruit was ready to cut up, and the Caesar salad ready to be thrown into a bowl. But now there would be no one to eat any of it. No homework to help the girls with. No hugs, snuggles, or kisses.

And no Noah.

Cassie chided herself for being silly. Good grief. It was only one night. She could handle being away from the Mackies for *one night*.

"Is everything okay?" Cassie asked. "With Noah, I mean?"

Becky waved off her concern. "I think that crazy woman who keeps changing her mind has struck again. Poor Noah. I'm sure he's more than ready to be done with that house."

185

Cassie nodded. "I could have still watched the girls. He didn't need to call you."

"He's probably going to be home late and wants them in their own beds."

Cassie could have driven over there and put them to bed. It wouldn't have been a problem at all. She glanced at the girls, feeling a strange reluctance to entrust them to anyone else—even Becky. Which was crazy. Adi and Kajsa weren't hers, and if there was an award for mother of the year, it would go to Becky. No question.

Adelynn finished changing and grabbed Cassie's hand. "Can't you come with us?" The hope in her beautiful brown eyes warmed Cassie's heart.

"She'll come another time," said Becky. "Tonight is Cassie's night to catch up."

Cassie did have a lot to catch up on, especially when it came to her job with Hansen Imaging. She crouched down and gave Adelynn a hug, then Kajsa. "I'll see you tomorrow, okay? And maybe this weekend we can go to the ranch."

They smiled and leapt and danced all the way out the door—even Kajsa. The moment they disappeared, though, loneliness echoed off the walls. She retrieved her phone from her bag, hoping to find a missed call from Noah so she'd have an excuse to call him back. But there was nothing. Not even a text.

Cassie had never complained about falling behind. She'd never given Noah any indication that watching the girls was too much for her because it wasn't. So why did Noah feel the need to ask Becky to step in, and why didn't he bother telling her about it? Did he really think she needed some time away from the girls? Or was it the girls who needed time away from her?

Cassie forced a smile as she said goodbye to the last of her students and their parents. Then she took her time cleaning up. When she was married to Landon, working and cleaning had become an outlet for her emotions. It didn't matter how she was feeling. Frustration, anger, hurt, sorrow—she'd shared all of it with the floor and dishes, mirrors and dusting cloths.

Around her, the floor suddenly looked filthy, the chairs disordered, and the glass a little foggy. Cassie yanked open the storage closet and got to work.

Noah glanced at his watch one more time. Only two minutes had passed since the last time he'd checked, but it felt like fifteen. Cassie's concrete porch steps were getting harder and colder, so he shifted positions and leaned forward, resting an elbow on his knees while he fiddled with a black bandana in his hands. What was taking her so long? His heels moved up and down, bouncing his arms as he squinted into the darkening sky for her white sedan. Did she need to stay late for something? Did she stop by the store? Go out for dinner?

Noah should have thought of those scenarios before he'd made the decision to surprise her. Becky could have hinted that she needed to go home right away—for . . . some reason.

He glanced down the street one more time, then leaned back on his elbows, making himself as comfortable as concrete steps would allow. Cassie would have to come home sooner or later, and he'd be right here when she did.

Twenty minutes later, when his eyes were beginning to drift closed, the sound of a car bumping into the driveway woke him up. *Finally.* He stifled a yawn as he sauntered over to her car, opening her door before she had a chance.

Her eyes widened when she saw him. "What are you doing here?"

"Waiting . . . and waiting . . . and waiting. Sheesh, what took you so long?"

"I was cleaning the studio." Her brow furrowed. "Becky said you had to work late. She took Adi and Kajsa and—"

"I know. I asked her to." He held out his hand, and when she made no move to take it, Noah reached for hers, easing her out of the car.

"Why?" she said. "If you ever have to work late, I can keep them. I can even go over to your house and put them to bed. I really don't mind. In fact—"

"Cass." He pulled her into his arms and breathed in the flowery scent of her hair. "I called Becky tonight because I'm being selfish and wanted you all to myself. I have a surprise for you."

"Surprise? Really?" She smiled, and her dimple appeared. "I love surprises."

"I hope you love being blindfolded too." He pulled the black handkerchief from his pocket and moved behind her. "Now close your eyes."

She twisted around with excited eyes. "Is the basement done?"

Noah rolled his eyes. "Do you have any idea how much effort—and patience—it took for me to try to surprise you tonight? The least you can do is pretend not to know what it is."

"But is it?"

He manually turned her back around. "Like I already told you," he said as he tied the blindfold around her head. "It's a *surprise*."

Once inside, she kicked off her shoes and latched on to his elbow. Noah smiled at the way she was too excited to hold still. He used to think she was so stiff and refined—incapable of letting go. But now he knew better. Underneath all that poise and polish was a complicated and vulnerable woman with a heart the size of Texas and a smile that brightened the world.

He dropped a kiss on her forehead, then led her carefully down the stairs.

"Ooh, the carpet is so soft. I love it."

At the bottom of the stairs, she lifted her nose and sniffed the air. "Something smells good," she murmured.

Noah glanced at the Chinese takeout boxes resting on a large blanket in the middle of the dance floor. "It would have tasted good too if you hadn't decided to go all neat freak on me." He moved behind her. "Ready?"

"Ready." The blindfold came off, and Cassie's eyes squinted as they adjusted to the light. Then they widened, and she looked around in awe. She ran her palm across the smooth, shiny surface of her new wooden floor. She opened closets, tested out the light switches, and made water spurt from the drinking fountain. She squished her toes into the soft carpet in the family room, brushed her fingers across the stone surrounding the fireplace, touched the mantle, and flipped a switch. The fire poofed to life, and she grinned.

Lastly, she checked out the bathroom. A quiet gasp sounded when she spotted the non-kitschy vanity that Noah had found and refinished in that antique glaze she loved.

He shuffled his feet, waiting. Did she like it? She stood with her back to him, staring at the one change he'd made without her permission. Maybe she hated it. Maybe she hated him for not running it by her first. But Noah had wanted to surprise her. The moment he'd spotted the vanity with it's simplistic, old world charm, he'd been so sure she'd love it.

But maybe he'd been wrong.

She turned around, and her eyes were filled with tears.

Good tears? Bad? "We can switch it out," he rushed to say. "I was hoping you'd like it. But if you don't, we can—"

She rushed forward and threw her arms around him with a half sob, half laugh. "I love it. I love it all. I love you." She rose to her tip toes and pressed her warm lips against his.

His mouth lifted into a smile that slowly faded as he kissed her back. His arms encircled her back, crushing her against him. Noah once thought that three dimensions were the most he could experience in this life. But when Cassie kissed him the way she was now, when the words "I love you," came from her mouth, his world unfolded to take on another dimension—a dimension that couldn't be seen, only felt, touched, tasted. And Noah felt everything. Her fingertips pressing into his back. Her body locked against his. Her soft lips that tasted like cherries. And something else— something that was happening inside him. Something warm, exciting, and good.

Noah used to think that he could never love anyone the way he'd loved Angie. But Cassie had shown him otherwise. With Angie, it had always been him and her or him and the girls. Their family had felt compartmentalized, like a house with too many walls and doors separating them. But with Cassie, there were no walls or closed doors. Everything was wide open and welcoming—big enough for the three of them. Big enough for anyone who wanted in.

Noah wanted that house. That floor plan. That life.

"Marry me, Cassie," he breathed against her lips. "Marry me."

Her fingers stiffened at the nape of his neck, her muscles tensed, and her mouth stopped moving against his. She pulled back and looked up at him. In her eyes, Noah saw a swirling mass of worry, confusion, and fear. There was no hope and joy. Only anxiety.

That's all it took for that extra dimension to shatter, plunging him into a one-dimensional world of black lines with no shapes or color. His hands slid from her face to his pockets, and he took a step back, not breaking eye contact. Two steps back and then three. When he was walking away, the anxiety in her expression didn't hurt him as much. That's when he wanted to see it, when he should see it. Only when he was walking away.

"Noah, please . . . try to understand. It's too soon . . . and I'm scared."

"Of what?" asked Noah. "Do you honestly think I've

been pretending to be something I'm not? That I'll turn into a version of Landon after we get married?"

"No, of course not."

"Then why are you scared?"

She shook her head, and her tears—once happy tears—dripped down her face like a leaky faucet. "I just need more time, that's all."

"More time for what?"

"To be sure." She sniffed and ran the back of her hand against her cheeks.

Noah looked away from the sorrow that filled her eyes. His jaw worked back and forth as he fought an internal battle to not argue. But it was hard. He wanted to put her on the witness stand and take on the role of a cross-examiner. He wanted to get to the bottom of her waffling and figure out exactly what made her so unsure. He wanted to prove her wrong; prove to her that what they had together may not be an absolute—because nothing was absolute—but it was as close to a sure thing as two people could get in this life.

Why couldn't she see that? Why couldn't she *believe* in that?

Cassie's hands felt cold as they closed over his. She squeezed them, bringing Noah's attention back to her. "I'm not saying no," she said. "Believe me, I want to say yes. More than anything, I want to say yes. There's no doubt in my mind I'm falling in love with you. But that's all I've been doing since I met you—falling. I need some time to land on solid ground again and . . . make sure."

Noah let out a breath as she wrapped her arms around him. He rested his chin on the top of her head and held her close. Yes, he could wait and be more patient. But what if Cassie never got there? What if she never landed on that solid ground?

He dismissed the thought the moment it arrived, refusing to believe that was even a possibility.

Cassie looked up at him. Her eyes and nose were a

blotchy shade of red that made her hair look almost orange. Noah smiled and wiped away the last of her tears with his thumbs.

"You'd better not break my heart," he said.

"I won't if you won't."

"Deal."

She pulled his head down to hers and kissed him lightly on the lips. Once, twice, thrice. Then she tucked her face into the crook of his neck and murmured, "Do you think that Chinese food is still okay to eat? Because I'm starving."

Noah squeezed her one last time before pulling her toward the blanket. "Let's go see."

"I really love our basement."

He stopped and glanced back. "*Our* basement?"

"Yes. Ours. You designed and built it. I just own it."

Noah smiled. "What about the vanity? Are you sure you love that too?"

"I really do. It's beautiful and not kitschy at all." She smiled. "Where did you get it?"

They sat down on the blanket, and Noah began opening Chinese take-out boxes. "Remember that crazy lady I'm working with right now?"

"How could I forget?"

"Well, she changes her mind on vanities too. She purchased that one from a small shop that didn't take returns, so I offered to buy it from her."

"Was it expensive?"

A low chuckle sounded. "It depends on how you look at it."

"What do you mean?"

"Let's just say she gave me a really good deal to make up for all the headaches she's given me. But if you count all the hours I've spent dealing with her and making all her changes, then yeah, it's very expensive."

Cassie laughed. "What did you do with the other one?"

"I listed it in the classifieds for free to the first person who could come and get it. Turns out there are a lot of people in this world who like kitschy things." He winked to show he was teasing.

"But not me," she clarified.

"No, thank goodness. Because what would that make me?"

She fingered the stubble across his chin. "Not kitschy, that's for sure."

Noah chuckled. They had such an easy camaraderie. They shared similar tastes—at least once Landon was out of the picture. They both loved Adi and Kajsa. They got along. They had a blast together. The chemistry between them was a force to be reckoned with. And they both liked cookie dough ice cream. How was this not a sure thing for her? He didn't understand.

Twenty-one

THE SLAM OF Noah's truck door echoed down the street, sounding loud in the quiet of the night. He started toward his house, then paused. The blinds were open, his front room light was on, and Becky was clinging to Justin with her phone clasped between her fingers. Justin was rubbing her back in a comforting gesture.

Only then did Noah remember that Kevin had tried to call.

He took the front porch steps two at a time and rushed inside. "What's wrong?"

Becky pulled free from her husband's arms and looked at him. "It's Emma," she said, her voice cracking. "She went into labor. Kevin said she was bleeding. He took her to the hospital thirty minutes ago, but I haven't heard anything else." She swallowed and shook her head. "I'm sorry for not calling, but I didn't want the girls to know, so I got them to bed first. Then I lost it and called Justin instead."

Noah kicked himself for not answering Kevin's call earlier. He'd been in the middle of dinner with Cassie and that had seemed more important than taking a call from his brother-in-law.

He should have answered.

Becky clasped Justin's hand and shook her head. "It's too early. She can't have those babies yet. And if they can't stop the labor . . . if the bleeding becomes dangerous . . ." Tears welled in her eyes. "They've waited so long, why this now? Why?"

"Shh," Justin said quietly, pulling her close once again. "It's going to be okay. They're going to stop the labor, and those babies are going to be just fine. You'll see."

Becky looked up with tear-streaked eyes. "How can you be sure?"

"I just know."

But he didn't know, not really. No one did. Noah dropped down on the armchair and leaned forward, placing his forehead in his hands and hating how out of control he felt. How out of control life in general could be. He'd learned from experience that people came into this world and then they left it. Sometimes they stayed for a while, sometimes not long at all, and sometimes only twenty-seven years.

Noah could only hope and pray that Emma and those babies had years of life ahead of them.

"We can stay here if you want to go to the hospital," said Becky.

As much as Noah wanted to be there for his sister, there wasn't much he could do sitting in a waiting room at the hospital. Nor was he about to leave Adi and Kajsa while the reminder of how precious life could be was staring him in the face. He wasn't going anywhere.

"You and Justin go," said Noah. "Just promise you'll call as soon as you hear anything."

"You sure?"

"I'm sure. I need to be here."

She nodded, then clasped Justin's hand and started forward, pausing when she reached the door.

"I almost forgot. How was your date tonight? Did Cassie love the basement?"

"It was good. And yes, she did. Thanks for keeping Adi and Kajsa for me."

"We had fun," she said, wiping her eyes again. "I've missed them."

"They've missed you too." Noah waved her off. "Now go. And don't forget to call."

"I won't." The door opened and closed, and the room suddenly became very quiet. Too quiet.

Noah grabbed the remote and turned on the TV. He flipped through several channels before he gave up and tossed it aside. Unable to sit any longer, he strode down the hall and quietly opened the door to Adi and Kajsa's room. As always, the room emanated a soft, peaceful glow—a peace he could really use right now. Adi was snuggled under her covers into a little ball with her head peeking out, and Kajsa had turned sideways on her bed, with her legs hanging over the edge.

Noah crept forward, carefully lifting her legs and swinging her around. Then he grabbed a pillow that had fallen on the floor and lay down in the middle of their room, willing the sound of their even breathing to lull his mind into a more peaceful state. Emma was going to be okay, she was. And those babies were going to be fine too. He tried so hard to know it, to feel it, to believe it, but the anxiety refused to go away.

Was this how Cassie felt about him? Was it this much of a struggle? This much worry and stress?

If there was one thing Noah had learned in his short life, it was that life happened. Whether good, whether bad, whether he made it happen or whether it happened all on its own, it just happened. And even though it may not seem okay at the time, eventually the pain subsided, the kinks got worked out, and weak people became a little stronger.

Eventually.

Maybe that's what Justin was referring to earlier, when he seemed so sure. Maybe that's what Cassie needed to learn and understand. Everything really was going to be okay.

The shrill ring of his phone made Noah lurch awake. He hit his head on Kajsa's bed frame and swallowed a curse as he yanked the phone from his pocket and turned off the sound. Then he escaped from the room and pulled the door closed behind him before answering the phone.

"Becky?"

"She's going to be okay," Becky said, sounding relieved. And tired.

"And the babies?" Noah clenched the phone in his fingers, waiting for news. Good news, he hoped.

"They were able to stop the bleeding and labor. For now, at least."

"For now? What does that mean?"

"It means they're going to monitor her for the next twenty-four hours, and if it stays stopped, they'll let her go home."

That sounded like a stupid idea to Noah. "But what if it doesn't stay stopped?"

"It should, as long as she stays in bed. At least that's the hope."

And then it all sank in. Bed rest. Emma could go home as long as she stayed in bed for the majority of every day until it was safe for those babies to come. He swallowed. "How did she take that news?"

"Let's just say that those little babies got their first scolding."

Noah chuckled, appreciating the release it gave him. "Can I talk to her?"

A shuffling noise sounded, followed by low murmurs,

and then Emma's voice. "Hey bro." She sounded more tired than Becky.

"You okay?" he asked.

"I'm okay." Her voice sounded quiet and withdrawn—so unlike Emma. And no wonder. For her, being confined to a bed all summer would be the equivalent to being stuck in an office all day for Noah. It would suck. He didn't envy her the next couple of months.

"I'm actually glad you're getting put on bed rest," said Noah, trying to sound upbeat and positive. "Now I can finally start paying you back for everything you've done for me during the past few years. We'll come visit and bring you dinner and help you clean and—"

Emma laughed. "I'm not sure I want your dinners. You're a worse cook than me. And while I appreciate the thought, I refuse to let you scrub my toilets. Wait, what was that, honey?" Emma's attention was pulled away for a moment, and then she returned. "Kevin just said he's going to hire a maid for me for the summer. Can you believe it? Me, having a maid. Imagine that."

"The next few months are going to fly by. Just wait and see. We'll take good care of you."

"I know you will." She paused. "It's not me I'm worried about. It's you."

"Me?" They must have given Emma morphine or something. She was clearly a little out of it.

"Well, Adi and Kajsa anyway," she said. "I won't be able to watch them this summer, and it's killing me."

Noah blinked. Had she been planning to do that? He let out a breath and sank down on the couch, suddenly exhausted. Of course she had. She was Emma. "I wasn't going to let you take them this summer—even before you got put on bed rest. You're pregnant with twins. You need to take care of yourself and stop worrying about everyone else."

"I know, but with Sam taking that internship and Becky's job getting busier in the summer months, I just—"

"Need to relax and know that I've got it covered."

"You do?"

"Yes," he lied. "I'm sorry I didn't tell you before now."

"Is Cassie . . . ?" She left the question hanging, probably because she knew it wouldn't be right to ask that of Cassie anymore than Noah did.

But he knew Emma. She wouldn't stop worrying until she knew the girls were okay. "Yes, she can help out. So don't worry."

A sigh sounded, and the tight edge to Emma's voice relaxed. "I'm so glad you have her now. She's been such a blessing."

"Yeah." Noah left it at that. Yes, he did have Cassie. Only he didn't. Not really. Not yet. "Let me know when they let you leave tomorrow."

"I will."

"Take care of yourself."

"You too."

Noah tossed the phone on the couch and bent forward, raking his fingers through his hair. What *was* he going to do about Adi and Kajsa? Summer was only a few weeks away and he still hadn't figured it out. Every time he considered hiring a stranger, his stomach twisted into knots. But he couldn't put it off any longer. Becky had mentioned that Sam had a friend who might be interested. Maybe he'd start there.

Twenty-two

"NOAH, IT'S SO great to finally meet you." Mrs. Fuller hugged Noah close, like he was already a part of their family. "We've heard so much about you from Cassie and the McCoys. I feel like I know you already. Come in, come in." She gestured inside her home. "Everyone is anxious to meet you."

Only then did Mrs. Fuller notice the two little girls standing nervously behind their daddy. "Oh my goodness!" Her warm smile spread even larger. She bent forward, lowering her head to their eye level. "You must be Adi and Kajsa. How beautiful you both are."

They smiled shyly, their eyes widening when they looked beyond Cassie's mother. The family room was full of people, voices, and laughter. Through the back window, a bunch of kids ran around the backyard.

Noah couldn't wait to meet everyone. During his time in Honduras, one of his best friends was number five in a family of ten kids. Even though their house was tiny, run down, and crammed, Noah could have spent every day there. Being surrounded by such a large group had made him feel like he was part of something bigger and greater and more important. Nobody messed with the Sandri kids because they'd be taking on the entire clan.

Cassie's large family, all clustered together, brought back memories of the Sandri family. Big, great, and wonderful. Some people yearned to marry into money, but not Noah. He wanted this—for both him and his girls.

"Vern Fuller." Cassie's dad was suddenly there, holding out his hand.

"Noah Mackie," said Noah, shaking his hand. "It's good to meet you, sir."

"Come on in. No need to stand out here all evening."

Noah took each of his daughters' hands and followed Cassie inside. The noise quieted down as introductions were made, and a lot of curious eyes took in the small Mackie family. Noah only remembered half of the names, but he'd never forget the feeling of closeness and camaraderie in that room. How could Cassie have stayed away for so long?

Her family made room for them on the loveseat, and Noah settled in, one daughter on each knee with Cassie at his side. Her parents asked some questions, her siblings followed up with some more, and then the ice officially broke and chaos resumed. Three different conversations struck up at once, squealing kids ran in and out, and somewhere, a dog barked.

"Noah." Vern folded his arms across his large chest. "I hear you know something about plumbing."

"*Dad.*" Cassie shot Noah an apologetic look before glaring at her father. "I already told you—no."

"No?"

"*No.*"

"Maybe Noah will say yes."

"No. He won't," she said firmly, looking back to Noah. "You won't."

"I might." Intrigued, Noah readjusted his girls and

shifted his legs to keep them from falling asleep. "What's the question? Or do I have to give you an answer first?"

Vern shifted in his seat. "Yesterday our toilet started leaking and—"

"Oh my gosh." Cassie dropped her forehead to her hands.

"And," her father repeated. "I was wondering if you'd take a look. I'm not sure what parts I need to get at the hardware store."

"I'd be happy to," said Noah.

"But not right now," Mary Ellen rushed to say. "I was just about to call everyone for dinner."

"After dinner then," said Noah.

Vern grunted in agreement, and Cassie leaned over to whisper, "You really don't have to."

"And I really don't mind. Why didn't you tell me before? I would have brought my tools."

"Because I didn't want you to have to bring your tools so you could fix my parents' toilet."

"But I like fixing things."

"Really?" said one of Cassie's brothers. Mark or Tyler? Noah couldn't remember. "Because my daughter has this dresser with drawers that are always getting stuck, and—"

"Seriously Mark?" Cassie hissed.

Ah, so his name is Mark. Noah committed the name and face to memory.

Mark shrugged. "What? He said he liked fixing things, and I happen to have something that needs fixing."

"He was only joking."

"No I wasn't," said Noah.

"No he wasn't," added Mark, pointing at Noah as if to say "See?"

Cassie stood and leveled Noah a look. "You are not going to fix my brother's dresser. He's a big boy and can do it himself." Noah laughed while she reached for Adelynn and

Kajsa's hands. "C'mon, let's go wash up before anyone else tries to add another project to your daddy's to-do list."

Dinner was a crazy, messy affair. Two cups of juice toppled, one plate piled high with grilled chicken and rice overturned, and a few kids ran through the messes before parents got a chance to clean it up. Voices had to be raised to be heard above all the other voices, and laughter sounded often.

Noah was ready to call them all family.

The girls finished eating and went outside with some of the other kids to play kickball. Noah watched from the back window until Vern reminded him about the leaky toilet. He withheld a grin as he followed Cassie's father to the bathroom and crouched down to examine the area that Vern pointed to.

"Do I need a new valve?"

Noah turned on the water and watched a few drops squeeze from one of the connections. He shut it back off and dried it with a washcloth. "I think all you need is a new compression ring. I'm pretty sure I have one hanging around somewhere if you want me to bring it by tomorrow on my way to work. It will only take a few minutes to switch this out for you."

"Oh, you don't need to go to all that trouble. I just wanted to know what I was dealing with."

"It's not a problem. I'll drop by in the morning. It'll be my way of saying thanks for a wonderful dinner."

"Well, offer accepted again. I'd appreciate that."

Noah returned to the front room and found Cassie on the couch chatting with a few of her siblings. He paused in the doorway, noting the easy way she talked and joked with them. There was no sign of awkwardness. Only happiness.

She glanced up and caught him watching. A soft smile lifted her lips, and she slid over to make room for him on the couch.

Noah sat beside her and rested his arm across the back

of the sofa. She snuggled next to him and lay her head on his shoulder, surprising him. He hadn't expected her to show any affection in front of her family, and yet here she was, cozying up to him and interlacing her fingers through his. Noah's arm slid from the back of the sofa to around her shoulders.

A few knowing looks passed between some of her siblings, but Noah didn't care.

Mary Ellen walked into the room, drying her hands on her apron. "Cassidy, did Monique ever get a hold of you? She called earlier this week for your phone number."

Lifting her head, Cassie cleared her throat. "Um, yeah. She called a few days ago."

"What did she want?"

Cassie directed a nervous glance at Noah before answering. "She, uh . . . was wondering if I'd be interested in teaching at her school's summer camp this year. One of the teachers quit suddenly, and she needs to fill the spot as soon as possible. The first session starts at the beginning of June, and she'll have to cancel one of the classes if she doesn't find a teacher."

"Haven't you already committed to teach summer classes at your own studio?" said her mother.

"Not this year. I planned to use the summer to get my basement set up and everything reorganized before starting up again in the fall."

"So what did you tell her?"

Cassie's hands fidgeted in her lap. "That I'd think about it."

Her sister, Michelle, walked in the room and settled on the armrest of the loveseat next to her husband. "Are you talking about Monique Sladen? I haven't seen her in years. Where is she these days, anyway?"

Noah was wondering the same thing—especially when Cassie shot him another uncertain look. "Um . . . Houston."

Houston? Noah's body went stiff. Cassie was thinking of going to Houston for the summer? Since when? And why was he just finding out about it now?

"Wow, that's kind of far away," said Mary Ellen. "Are you really considering it?"

"I don't know," said Cassie. "She could really use my help, and I'm one of the few people she's contacted who could make it work. So . . . I don't know." Cassie fiddled with a ring on her finger—a ring she hadn't received from Noah. Which meant she was free to go. Or free to not go. Or free to do whatever she wanted without telling him anything, which was exactly what she'd done.

Noah removed his arm from around her shoulders, clasped his hands together, and leaned forward to get a better look at her.

"I was going to tell you." She was speaking to him now. With her entire family watching for his reaction.

Noah kept his mouth shut. If he opened it, something snarky like "Before or after you made your decision?" would have slipped out. He chose to nod instead. Nod and breathe and try his hardest not to think or feel.

No one spoke, which made for an uncomfortable silence in a room filled with people. Noah shifted in his seat. If this was what it was like when Cassie first came back after Landon's funeral, no wonder she didn't want a repeat experience. The whole "big family" thing suddenly seemed overrated.

"I should check on the girls," he blurted, standing. Maybe the backyard would have less dense air.

"And I should check on the dessert," Mary Ellen said right after. Evidently she wasn't a fan of tension either.

Cassie tried to reach for his hand, but Noah evaded her grip, taking long strides across the room. He couldn't get out of there fast enough. In the backyard, he found his girls tossing a playground ball with one of Cassie's nephews.

Noah intercepted the ball. "Mind if I join in?"

"Only if you throw it to me," said one nephew, pointing to Adi. "She throws like a girl."

"Stop making fun of me!" His daughter stomped her foot, glaring at the boy who was about her age. "I throw like a girl because I *am* a girl."

"Yeah, but you don't have to throw like one."

"And you don't have to be a stupid head," cried Adi, clearly offended.

Whoa. It looked like Noah had just traded one uncomfortable situation for another.

"You can't even kick a ball straight," the boy taunted.

"Yes. I. Can!" Adi took the ball from Noah, set it on the ground, and kicked it as hard as she could. Instead of going forward, it flew sideways toward Kajsa, who actually caught it.

The boy started cackling and pointing a finger. "Told you." He doubled over he was laughing so hard.

"She might not kick straight, but I can." Kajsa glared at the boy then drop-kicked the ball. He had to duck to keep from getting nailed in the face.

Noah couldn't help but feel impressed. Kajsa had been holding out on him. She had some skills.

The boy wasn't laughing any longer. He retrieved the ball, glared at Kajsa, and retracted his arm, getting ready to hurl it at her.

Noah jumped forward, ready to intercept, when a female voice shouted from behind. "Alexander Christian Overton, you put down that ball and come here this second."

He pointed at Kajsa. "But she tried to hit me."

"I don't care what she tried to do. Kajsa is a guest, and we don't throw balls at guests."

"But—"

"Come here." She pointed at the ground near her feet. "Now."

The boy shot one last glare at Kajsa before dropping the

ball and stalking toward his mother. Behind her, Cassie slipped out the back door and approached Noah.

"Is everything okay?"

Noah wasn't sure if she was referring to the girls or to him. "I think it's time for us to go," he said.

"Oh, okay. Let me get my purse."

Noah didn't waste any time ushering his girls inside. "Thank you so much for dinner," he told Mary Ellen as he walked through the kitchen. "It was wonderful."

"You're not staying for dessert? I'm just about to pull it out of the oven."

"Thank you, but we have some stuff we need to get done. And the girls have school tomorrow."

She nodded, her warm eyes understanding. "It was really good to meet you. Don't be a stranger."

Noah smiled then nodded a goodbye to everyone else as he crossed back through the house. "I'll see you tomorrow morning, Vern. I won't forget."

Cassie's father patted him on the back. "It's much appreciated, son."

Son. Ten minutes earlier, the term would have been high praise. But Noah felt less like a son now than when he'd first arrived.

Twenty-three

CASSIE FIDGETED THE entire drive back to her house. Noah was upset with her, and he had every right to be. Surrounded by her family—in her parents' home—was not the place he should have found out about Monique's offer. She should have told him before.

Could've, would've, should've.

Only didn't.

And now his two daughters occupied the back seat, making a much needed conversation impossible.

He pulled to a stop in her driveway and waited, not bothering to even look her way. Cassie tried to stamp down the pain. It was her fault she was getting the cold shoulder.

"Thanks for coming with me today," she said weakly.

"No problem."

Not knowing what else to say, Cassie opened her door and stepped one foot out. She hesitated, looking over her shoulder at Adelynn and Kajsa. "I'll see you soon." She mustered a smile and blew them each a kiss. Then she glanced at Noah, and her smile faded. "I'll call you tonight."

He nodded, still looking straight ahead.

Forcing her body to move, Cassie got out and closed the door. She watched as Noah's truck pulled out of the driveway and rumbled away.

Her heart felt heavy and her stomach clenched. Hurting Noah was the last thing she'd wanted to do.

But he'd proposed. *Proposed!* Cassie had just gotten comfortable with dating him, and he had to go and throw that out there like it was the next logical step.

Meet. Check.

Get to know each other. Check, check, check.

Propose. Check.

Only Cassie wasn't ready to check off that next box. There were way too many other checks that needed to happen under the Get to Know Each Other category. Lots of checks. Hundreds and thousands of checks.

Why did Noah have to be in such a hurry? He needed to watch *What About Bob?* and learn about baby steps. He needed to read *The Tortoise and the Hare* and understand the concept of slow and steady. He needed to let life play out at a normal speed and not feel the need to keep pressing Fast Forward.

When Monique had called, her offer had felt like an answer to prayer. Cassie could accept it, spend the summer in Houston, and she and Noah would be forced to take a few steps back and slow things down. It would be good for them. It would be good for her.

But how could she make Noah understand that without hurting him? She couldn't. Which was why she'd said nothing. Which was also why she hadn't accepted the offer yet.

Only now everything had backfired, and Cassie wanted nothing more than to click Undo on this entire day. If only that was an option.

Cassie passed the time by cleaning. She dusted every exposed surface in her house, vacuumed, polished, scrubbed, and mopped. She straightened and organized—even going so far as to stack the ice cream containers neatly in her freezer. But then it reminded her more of Landon and less of Noah, so she toppled them over and closed the door before any of them could fall out.

When she'd finished with the main level, she wandered down to the basement. But as she looked around at everything Noah had created, it reminded her too much of him, how good he'd been to her, and how not-good she'd been to him. So she jogged back upstairs and dusted the family room a second time.

By the time nine o'clock rolled around, Cassie was through waiting. She picked up the phone to call, then shoved it back in her purse and slipped on her shoes instead. The usual ten minute drive to his house took seven.

The light was still on in Adi and Kajsa's room, so Cassie waited in her car. When it finally flicked off, and a duller glow took its place, she forced herself to wait an additional twenty minutes. Then she walked to the door and knocked quietly. And waited some more.

When another knock still left her waiting, Cassie pulled out her phone and called Noah. It rang three times before going to voicemail. Normally, it rang five times, which meant he'd rejected her call. Apparently, he wasn't ready to talk.

Well, Cassie was. She'd driven all this way, and she was going to find a way to make this right whether he liked it or not. So she walked around the side of the house to the outside of his window and knocked.

Moments later, a crack in the blinds appeared, and Noah squinted out at her. "We need to talk," she mouthed at him.

He looked away for a second then nodded. The blinds closed, and Cassie made her way back to the front door where she waited until Noah opened it and let her inside. He closed the door, leaned his back against it, and folded his arms, watching her expectantly.

Cassie suddenly felt unprepared. She'd been thinking all day about how she'd explain. She'd formed hundreds of sentences meant to make things right, but now—with him watching her like that—all those words and explanations evaporated. She had no idea where to begin. And from the look of Noah's tight jaw, he wasn't about to step in and help her out.

"I was going to tell you," she finally blurted—er, repeated. She'd already said as much at her parents' house.

"When? After you'd already decided?"

"Yes." When his jaw tensed, Cassie belatedly realized how that sounded. "I mean, no. I mean, I was ninety percent sure I was going to turn it down, so what was the point in bringing it up when—"

"What was the point?" Noah pushed away from the door, his eyes zeroing in on hers. "The point *is*, we're in a relationship now. And this is the kind of thing we should talk about *before* any decisions are made—be it ninety percent sure or ten percent."

He was right, of course.

"I'm sorry," was her only explanation.

"Yeah? Well, me too." He stood in front of her, his arms still folded. "Were you afraid I'd try to stop you from going? Is that it?"

"No. Of course not."

"Then why didn't you tell me? You totally blindsided me in front of your entire family, Cass, and I'd really like to understand what's going on inside your head."

Even though they were standing in the middle of the room, Cassie felt like she was being backed into a corner. "I don't know." She fidgeted again. "I guess I didn't think it was that big of a deal."

"You spending the summer in Houston is not that big of a deal?"

"Not if I'm not going."

Noah let out a breath as though his patience was nearing an end. "Tell me this. You said you were ninety percent sure you were going to turn it down. What was that extra ten percent thinking?"

Now he'd really backed her into a corner with no way out—other than to tell the truth, which was something she absolutely did not want to do.

"Monique needs my help," she finally said. "I feel bad leaving her in a bind."

"But isn't that what you've been doing since she called? If you're really planning on turning her down, she'll now have even less time to find someone else."

Cassie was running out of excuses. Actually, she was out of them. She sank down on the chair, feeling exhausted all of a sudden. "I know. I'm going to call her in the morning and tell her I can't make it."

Noah took a seat opposite her and leaned forward, resting his chin on his fingers. "Do you want to go to Houston, Cassie?"

"No." That much was true. She had no desire to be away from him or the girls for the summer. She just thought it would be good for them. And sometimes, the things that made a relationship stronger were the harder paths to take.

"Then why did you tell her you wanted to think about it? And don't give me that garbage about not wanting to leave her in a bind. There are other dance teachers out there."

It was the moment Cassie had hoped to avoid. The moment she could say "I don't know" and pray he'd accept that as an answer even though it wasn't one, or the moment she could tell him the truth and risk hurting him even more.

But what good was a relationship where honesty didn't exist?

Her eyes pled with Noah's to understand. "I told her I wanted to think about it because I think the separation would do us both some good."

Noah said nothing. He just blinked at her. Finally, he opened his mouth to say something then snapped it shut.

Cassie moved to sit beside him and clasped his hand in hers. "Noah, from the day we met, we've gone from zero to sixty in what feels like two seconds, and it's too fast. People can't know each other well enough in that short of time. The last time I rushed into something, it ended in disaster. I don't want that to happen to us."

Noah's nostrils flared slightly, and his jaw worked back and forth. Cassie shriveled inside. Why hadn't she stuck with "I don't know"? Why had she thought that honesty would be a good idea? Because it wasn't. If the truth hurt, then people should just keep their mouths shut.

"I'm not Landon," he finally said, his voice hard.

"I know."

"Then why do you keep comparing us? It's like you're looking for similarities—any reason why we shouldn't be together—and when you come up empty, you try harder. And I'm sick of it. I've never been anyone other than myself, and if you don't know by now that we're not headed for disaster, then maybe you never will."

It sounded so final. Like he was ready to call it quits here and now. How had it come to this? "That's not what I'm saying at all. I—"

Noah pulled his hand free and walked to the door, opening it. "I think you're right. I think you should call Monique, accept her offer, and spend the summer in Texas. Maybe by the time you come back, you'll know what it is you really want."

Cassie shook her head, refusing to walk out the door. "Please, let's talk about this."

"I'm all talked out." He glanced at her, and in his eyes she saw sorrow. Defeat. "I know I love you. I know I want to marry you. I know I want to spend my life with you. It's *you* who needs to figure things out, not me. So don't tell me that a few months of separation will do us both good when I already know what I want. The question is: What do you want? If you can tell me right now what it is, I'll listen. If not, I think you should go to Houston and figure it out."

He'd basically given her an ultimatum. Stay here and make plans to marry him or go to Houston. But if she did go, if she left things like this, what would happen to them? Would there even be a them?

Cassie didn't know. She didn't know anything anymore.

Slowly, she stood and walked toward him. She placed her hand on his chest and felt the rhythm of his heartbeat. It was so sure, so strong, so confident. Like him. Noah deserved confidence to be met with confidence and faith to be met with faith. He deserved the kind of love he gave, and until Cassie could give him that without fear or reservation, it would always be unequal. And that wasn't fair to him.

"It's not that I think we're headed toward disaster," she said in a small voice. "I think we're headed toward something stunning and wonderful. I just want us to take our time getting there. That's all."

His eyes met hers. "You're forgetting that stunning and wonderful can be taken away at the drop of a hat. So why not snatch it up while we can and enjoy it for as long as possible?"

"Because I'm not ready," she said quietly. Strong and lasting relationships took time to grow, like her aunt and uncle's. She pushed up to her tiptoes and pressed a kiss to his scruffy cheek, then dropped down to the balls of her feet, willing him to understand.

"I hope you have a great time in Texas. I really do."

He was saying goodbye. Cassie didn't want him to say goodbye. Not like this. She wanted him to say that they'd talk soon, that he'd call her every day. That even though they'd be a few states apart, they would still continue to grow closer. Just at a slower, more sedate pace.

A lump formed in Cassie's throat. It hurt to swallow. It hurt to breathe. It hurt to stand there and watch Noah, feeling like she was letting him slip through her fingers.

Before the tears could come, she turned and walked away, not knowing whether she was being wise or making the biggest mistake of her life.

Pain was like a sledgehammer. It was a destroyer. With one or two hard strokes, it could tear apart something whole and turn it into ugly chunks and pieces. With every step Cassie took away from him, Noah felt himself crumble.

She'd chosen to leave. Why? Because the separation would do them good; because the congested and humid Houston air would somehow clear her head.

Well, maybe it would. Maybe she'd come back ready to commit, maybe she'd come back still wanting more time, or maybe she wouldn't come back at all.

The question was: Would he still be waiting when she did come back?

Noah wandered down the hall, pausing outside his daughters' door. He cracked it open and watched his two beautiful girls. Kajsa rolled to her side, mumbling something in her sleep, and Adelynn was dead to the world. They were both so good, so sweet, so loving. There was no holding back with either of them, and he loved that.

Why couldn't Cassie be the same? Why did everything have to be so hard with her? So much work?

The greatest rewards in life aren't easily earned.

His father's words came to Noah's mind like another blow. He didn't want to think about them or believe them. Falling in love should be different. It should be easy, the way it had been with Angie. If it was right, everything should be smooth sailing.

Without rocky waves, how can you appreciate calm waters?

Stop it, Dad! Noah wanted to cover his ears with his hands and block out that voice, that advice, that wisdom.

Instead, he closed his girls' door and went to his room. Noah had seen so much in his life. He'd seen people get knocked down, sickness take kids from parents, and homes get torn apart by winds and floods. But he'd also seen people pick themselves up and move forward with purpose. He'd seen resolve follow tragedy and joy follow heartache. He'd seen people become better and stronger.

Noah had a beautiful home and a little money in the bank. He had two healthy daughters brimming with talent and promise. And until Cassie said otherwise, he chose to think that he still had her.

All he needed to do now was pick himself up and move forward, knowing, like with Emma and her babies, that everything really would be okay.

Twenty-four

LET'S TRY IT one more time," Cassie said to the ten little girls staring back at her. All wore black shorts and red shirts with Monique's School of Irish Dance scribbled across the front. They looked so darling and uniform. In the two weeks Cassie had been teaching, she'd learned so much from Monique about professionalism and how she wanted her own school to run. When Cassie got home, the first thing she'd do was locate a designer to create a logo for her school. Then she'd have uniforms made, and maybe by next year, she'd be ready to offer a summer program as well.

Cassie moved her feet slowly, showing the girls the steps while repeating them out loud. "Shuffle, hop back, and one-two-three. Yes, just like that." Some of the girls could do it, some of them came close, and some of them didn't come close at all. The discrepancy between their abilities reminded Cassie so much of Kajsa and Adelynn that a lump lodged in her throat, refusing to budge no matter how many times she swallowed or tried to focus on her class.

"Okay, everyone, it's time to cool down."

The girls all dropped to the ground for their stretches. Cassie watched Stevie, a little girl with brown hair and blue eyes, try so hard to reach her toes but not quite make it. From this angle, she looked a lot like Kajsa. Was Stevie horse crazy too?

Stop it, she told herself. *Focus.*

But, like every other day, her thoughts refused to stray far from a rough-around-the-edges, cookie-dough-loving guy and his two precious daughters.

The passage of time was supposed to make things easier, wasn't it? Time heals all wounds and all that. Why then, did the emptiness keep growing and tearing inside her? Cassie didn't laugh the way she did with Noah. She didn't smile the same or feel the same. She wasn't the same. Houston was a bustling, crowded place, with so much to see and do. But without Noah and Adi and Kajsa there to experience it with her, everything felt dull and lifeless. Cassie was back to being an empty geode, with no sparkles or color. And it stunk.

After all the parents had come and gone, Cassie stretched her arms behind her, trying to relieve the ache in her shoulders and the onset of a headache.

"Hey, girl." Monique's head appeared through the open door, her tight, black curls splaying around her beautiful, dark face. Monique was one of the few people who never had to wear a bun wig for performances. She simply pulled her hair up in a high ponytail, and it was as curly as everyone else's. "Want to see a play tonight at the Alley? A bunch of us are going."

"What play?" Cassie asked.

"*The Foreigner,* I think. It's supposed to be a riot."

Every night, Monique had something fun planned. Whether it was an Astro's game, a progressive dinner, or a concert in the park, she made it her mission to see that Cassie made the most of her summer in Houston. Normally, Cassie agreed, thinking busyness was the best way to keep her mind off the Mackie family. But tonight, she couldn't muster the will.

"If it's okay with you, I think I'm going to pass. I feel a killer headache coming on, and I think I could really use a night in."

"Shoot. I'm sorry. I hate headaches. But I have to go home and change anyway, so we can at least ride the metro together."

"Okay. Let me grab my stuff."

Cassie slung her bag over her shoulder and followed her friend outside. She'd been here two weeks already, and every time she walked outside, the hot and sticky air wrapped around her like a heavy, uncomfortable blanket.

"Can you believe the first summer session is almost halfway over?" said Monique as she locked up.

"No." Though it wasn't because time had flown by like Monique implied. It was because Cassie had thought the first two weeks would never end. It was now the middle of June, and she'd been in Texas for sixteen days. But it had been about a month since she'd seen or talked to Noah. It felt like a lifetime ago—like she'd return at the end of the summer to find him with gray hair, wrinkles, and grandchildren.

"Have I told you how grateful I am that you're here?" said Monique, giving Cassie a one-armed hug as they dodged all the people on the sidewalk. "I have no idea what I would have done without you."

"You would have found someone else," said Cassie. "Anyone would be crazy to turn down the chance to spend the summer in this lovely weather."

Monique laughed. "Isn't that the truth. Bless you for coming. I couldn't share my apartment with just anyone, you know."

Cassie smiled and shook her head, but her thoughts were miles away. Nine hundred and fifty-seven to be exact. She'd looked it up the moment she'd stepped off the plane.

"Hey, you okay?" Monique asked after they'd boarded the metro. "You don't seem like yourself."

"Sorry. It's just this headache. I'll be better tomorrow."

"You sure that's all it is?"

"Yeah." Cassie mustered a smile. "Tell me about this play and what I'm going to be missing."

Monique launched into a description of all the things she'd heard and read about the new play that had recently opened.

Cassie tried to listen, but as they moved along the rail, her senses felt deprived. She missed the smell of the dry Colorado Springs air, the sound of her hard shoes echoing off her shiny new wood floor, and seeing Adi and Kajsa's smiles. But mostly, she missed Noah. She wanted to hear him, see him, touch him, smell him, and taste him.

"It's our stop." Monique's voice pried Cassie away from her self-pitying thoughts. They exited the car, and Monique continued to prattle the rest of the way back to her apartment. Then she quickly changed, grabbed a banana off the counter, and was off in a flurry of energy.

The moment the door closed, Cassie leaned against the back of the small, cherry red sofa. Outside, horns blared, voices shouted, and engines roared, but the apartment had never felt quieter. Cassie looked around, wondering what to do. Read a book? Take a bubble bath? Watch a movie? Go to sleep early so she could cross one more day off her calendar? Too bad she wasn't remotely tired.

She pushed away from the sofa and yanked open the freezer door, grabbing the half-gallon-sized container of cookie dough ice cream she kept for her missing-Noah-like-crazy moments. It made her feel closer to him somehow. She liked to imagine him eating the mint version and thinking of her at the same time. She pressed the frozen container against her perspiring forehead as she grabbed a spoon from the drawer.

After the second bite, a ringing sounded, and for a

second, Cassie thought it was coming from outside. But then she realized it was her phone. Almost frantically, she dropped the spoon and dug through her purse, searching for it like it was a lifeline. When her fingers finally closed around it, she pulled it out, hoping she'd see Noah's name on the screen. But it wasn't him.

She tried to keep the disappointment out of her voice as she answered. "Hey, Mom."

"I'm just calling to check in on you," said her mother. "I haven't heard from you this week."

"Sorry. Monique keeps me busy," said Cassie. "But things are good."

"You don't sound good."

"It's only because I have a headache."

A pause. "It sounds worse than a headache."

Her mother was too perceptive. "Okay, so maybe I'm feeling a little homesick tonight. But that's normal, right?"

"Homesick for whom?"

"My family."

"Which one?"

"Ours. Yours. Dad's. The only family I have."

"Liar."

"Mom!"

"Honey, I'm sorry, but you went two years without much contact with any of us. You can't really expect me to believe that after only two weeks you're homesick."

Cassie slumped against the back of her chair. She really hated it when her mother called her out like this.

"You miss Noah, don't you?"

"Maybe."

A quiet chuckle sounded. "Honey, what are you doing there? I mean, really."

"I'm getting away. I'm giving us a much needed break."

"I didn't realize you were in need of a break."

Cassie was quiet. She hadn't told anyone about Noah's impromptu proposal and wasn't sure she wanted to. But how

221

else could she explain? "Things were just moving . . . too fast."

"You were only dating."

"He proposed, Mom," the words came out before Cassie could swallow them whole. Why had she said that?

Silence. And then, "When?"

"A while ago. Before you met him. Which is the whole point. He hadn't even met my family and he proposed. Who does that?"

"Your father."

"What?"

Her mom chuckled again. "It only took him five weeks."

"Are you joking?"

"Nope."

Why hadn't Cassie heard this before? Why hadn't she asked? "What did you say?"

"Yes, of course. I was head over heels in love with that man. And we were married two months later."

Two months plus five weeks equaled just over three months. Her mom had only known her dad for *three months*? Cassie suddenly felt like she'd just discovered a deep, dark, family secret. "What did Aunt Jane say?"

"She thought I was crazy. And maybe I was. But being in love makes you do crazy things, and that's okay. I kind of like how my life turned out."

Cassie breathed in deeply, allowing this new revelation to settle in her mind. Her parents were so good together. So happy. So *lucky*. Not many couples could get away with dating only three months and still be married forty years later.

"How did you know it would last?"

"I didn't," her mother answered. "I knew I loved him. I knew he made me happy. I knew I connected with him in a way I'd never connected with anyone else. I knew I wanted to marry him. And that was it. The rest we had to work out along the way."

"You didn't feel like it was all happening too fast?"

"Of course I did. I nearly backed out three or four times."

"Dad too?"

"Heavens no. You know your father. Once he makes a decision there's no changing his mind. He decided he wanted to marry me, and that was that."

"Wow." *Like mother, like daughter.* "If you were that nervous about it, why did you go through with it?"

A heavy sigh sounded on the other line. "Honestly? I had no reason not to. There were no red flags with your father. He was a good man, and I loved him. So I took a leap of faith and married him. Scariest day of my life."

Cassie laughed, but when thoughts of her failed marriage invaded, she soon sobered. "I didn't think there were any red flags with Landon either."

"Oh, there were plenty. Believe me. You just didn't want to see or hear about them from anyone else."

Wasn't that the truth. Cassie had been so blind. So naïve. So ready to walk down the aisle and say "I do" to the man of her dreams. But everything about Landon had been superficial. Cassie's dreams had been superficial. Find a handsome, debonair man, and it will follow that he's also kind and good and wonderful.

Yeah right.

"Cassie?" Her mom's voice cut into her thoughts. "You still there?"

"Sorry. I was just thinking about how stupid I used to be."

"'Used to' being the operative phrase."

Once again, her mother was right. From the beginning with Noah, Cassie had looked for more in him than suave or debonair. She'd looked for depth and sincerity and humor and kindness. His hard work ethic had impressed her, along with the close relationship he had with his daughters. Noah was the whole package. The whole, red-flagless package.

Nothing should be keeping her from saying yes and walking down that aisle.

Nothing.

So why *was* she here?

"He called the other day," said her mother.

"Who? Noah?"

"Yes. He was wondering if I knew of anyone who might be interested in watching his daughters for the summer. I guess his current sitter isn't working out."

Cassie sat up straighter. "What about Emma and Becky?"

"Who?"

"His sister and neighbor."

A pause. "He didn't say anything about them. Only that he needed someone to start next week. That's all I know. I felt terrible because I couldn't think of anyone. After all he's done to help us fix things around the house over the past several weeks, I—"

"Mom, I'm sorry, but I've got to go," said Cassie as she slammed the lid back on the ice cream. "I have to make some calls."

"To Noah?"

Cassie smiled at the hope in her mother's voice—hope that had never been there with Landon. "No. I need to find another teacher for my class so Monique doesn't kill me. I'm coming home."

Twenty-five

NOAH DROVE HOME from work as fast as he dared. One of the more talkative homeowners had dropped by the job site at quitting time and engaged Noah in conversation. He'd tried to be polite, but after twenty minutes and still no wrapping up in sight, Noah had finally excused himself.

The light ahead of him turned yellow, and Noah punched on the gas, breezing through the intersection as it turned red. He rubbed his bleary eyes, hating that he was late. Hating that homeowner for making him late. And hating the fact that Adi and Kajsa didn't like their new babysitter.

In the two weeks since summer vacation had begun, his daughters had been through two. Sam's friend had been the first attempt, but she'd been more interested in socializing with her friends than playing with his daughters. So he'd replaced her with the niece of one of Becky's clients—Kelly, a girl who felt the need to text him about every little thing.

Kajsa wants to wear her boots to the park. Is that okay?

Adi spilled grape juice all over the family room floor.

225

How do I get it out?

Kajsa and Adi want to go to their Aunt Emma's for a few minutes. Can I let them?

Noah couldn't handle all the interruptions anymore—or the concern that Adi and Kajsa would sneak off to Emma's because they'd rather be with a bed-ridden aunt than the babysitter.

His truck lurched into the driveway and squealed to a halt. Seconds later, he was out the door and in his house.

"Sorry I'm late," he blurted before he realized he was talking to no one. The front room and kitchen were empty.

Voices and giggles sounded from down the hall, and Noah hesitated. Giggles? Did he really just hear his girls giggle? Were they actually having fun with Kelly? Come to think of it, Noah hadn't gotten a text from her anytime in the past—he glanced at his phone—two hours. Was it a sign that Kelly might actually work out?

Please yes.

Not wanting to disrupt what sounded like a happy moment, Noah walked quietly down the hall, pausing outside his girls' door. Through the crack, he saw the backs of three heads from the other side of Kajsa's bed—one blond, one brown, and one strawberry blond. Was Kelly's hair that color? Noah couldn't remember, which was strange, because it looked so much like Cassie's that he would have noticed.

"This is me at this really cool mall called The Galleria. And that's Monique hanging from a tree in a huge park called Memorial Park. You should see it. It makes your neighborhood park look teeny tiny."

Noah froze. Cassie was here. Now. Six weeks ahead of schedule. Was Noah imagining things?

"It's kind of blurry, but that's me in front of the Water Wall. It's the largest, man-made fountain in America. It's pretty amazing."

"What's that?" Kajsa said, pointing to something on Cassie's phone.

"Only the most amazing burger place ever. One day I'm going to take you both there so you can try their steak fries. But not during the summer. We'll go in January when the climate is more reasonable."

"Will you really take us?" asked Adi. "All the way to Texas?"

"Of course, silly." Cassie tickled her, and another giggle sounded. "I never make promises I don't intend to keep. Maybe we can go to a play while we're there."

"Can Daddy come too?"

Cassie paused, and her voice quieted. Noah had to strain to hear the words. "I would love it if he did."

Something that felt like hope swelled in Noah's heart. He pushed the door open all the way, and a floorboard creaked when he stepped inside the room. All three heads spun to face him.

"Daddy!" Adelynn hopped up on the bed, looking happier than he'd seen her since summer vacation began. "Look who's here."

"Guess what?" Kajsa said. "Cassie got to go on a horseback ride through the country. I'm so jealous."

"Pretty crazy," Noah said with his eyes locked on Cassie. She looked beautiful with her hair framing her face in soft, silky curls. He wanted to run his fingers through it and hold her close.

But why was she here? Was this just a weekend trip home?

Cassie stood and nervously smoothed down her denim skirt. "Why didn't you tell me Emma was put on bed rest?"

"Um . . ."

"He got strangers to watch us," Adelynn said, sounding outraged. "*Strangers.*"

"They wouldn't have been strangers for long if they'd done a decent job," Noah muttered.

Cassie walked around the bed and stopped in front of him. "You should have called. I would have—"

"What? Walked out on Monique?"

"Yes. That's exactly what I would have done—what I did do. My mom called. I came as soon as I heard."

So that's why she was back early. Not because she'd figured things out or wanted to come back but because she felt the need to bail him out. Noah took a step back and shoved his hands into his pockets. "I wish you wouldn't have done that. We're doing just fine."

"I was going to come back anyway," she blurted. "Even if you didn't need me, I was going to come home."

"Why?"

She tentatively stepped closer. "To apologize."

Noah wasn't sure how to think or feel. All he knew was Cassie was standing in front of him, telling him she would have come back regardless. What did that even mean? "For what?"

"For not seeing."

"Not seeing what?" Adelynn said. "Do you need glasses, Cassie?"

She smiled, revealing that dimple he loved. "In a way, I did need glasses, Adi. But not anymore. Now I see very clearly. And what I see, I love."

"You're looking at Daddy," said Adelynn.

"I know."

Noah's heart pounded like a jackhammer. Cassie picked up one of his hands and then another, threading her fingers through his as she stepped in closer. She smelled the same, looked the same, felt the same—but in her eyes Noah saw a confidence that hadn't been there before. It warmed him from the inside out.

"Are you going to kiss her?" said Kajsa. "Because that's gross."

Noah glanced at his interruptive daughters. "Your dance teacher and I need a few minutes alone, if that's okay. Why don't you two . . ." He paused, looking around the room for something they could do. Coming up empty, he grabbed his phone from his pocket and tossed it on Kajsa's bed. "Play with that while Cassie and I, uh . . . talk."

The two girls lunged for the phone as Noah pulled Cassie from the room. He led her down the hall and into the family room. His hands cradled her face as he looked into her eyes.

"My answer is yes." She smiled shyly at him. "If the question's still on the table, my answer is yes. I love you, Noah Mackie, and I want to spend the rest of my life with you."

"You sure?" he said, not quite believing she could be. "Because you know how it works with me. Once I'm upgraded, that's that. There's no downgrading allowed."

"I'm absolutely, one hundred percent sure."

Noah didn't waste another second. His smiling mouth covered hers in a kiss that conveyed how he felt about his new fiancé status. Her arms locked around his shoulders in a vise-like grip, and her mouth moved against his with passion and hunger, like a woman who knew exactly what she wanted. It all felt like a dream; as though he'd wake up any moment to find her back in Texas, still doubting their future together.

But this wasn't a dream. It was real. She was real. Cassie was now his to have, to hold, to treasure.

"Can we come out now, Daddy?" Adi called from down the hall.

"No," he said, his lips moving to Cassie's neck.

She sighed and leaned into him.

"Please?" Adi's voice called again.

"No," he said again, returning to her lips.

"But Kajsa's calling Aunt Emma, and I'm bored."

A giggle escaped Cassie's mouth, and Noah reluctantly pried himself away. Only then did Adelynn's words register. "Wait, Kajsa is calling who?"

"She's asking Aunt Emma if we can come over so we don't have to stay in our room like *prisoners*."

Noah rolled his eyes. That's what he got for leaving his phone with them.

"Aunt Emma says to come over right now!" Kajsa's voice sounded, and the two girls ran from their room, only to be stopped by Noah in the hallway. "Sorry, but you know the rules. You can't go over there without me."

"But she said you need some time alone with Cassie and we should hurry as fast as we can. Oh, and she said to tell you that Uncle Kevin's home so don't worry." She grinned at her sister. "He's going to make us corn on the cob for dinner."

"Please, Daddy?" Adelynn's large brown eyes turned puppydog-ish. "It's corn on the cob. My *favorite*."

Everything that Kevin cooked was his daughter's favorite. But if Kevin and Emma were going to invite his daughters over, Noah wasn't going to argue.

"Go ahead." He stepped out of their way and let them go. As soon as the front door slammed, his mouth lifted into a smile. His hands found Cassie's waist, and he pulled her close. "Remind me to thank my sister."

"You should thank your sister."

"I meant later."

"Oh." She wound her arms around his neck, twirling her fingers in his hair. "I wonder what we should do now."

"We should celebrate."

"Celebrate what?"

Noah dropped a kiss on the tip of her nose. "The fact that you're no longer blind as a bat."

"Now that's romantic," she said dryly.

A chuckle rumbled inside his chest, and as Noah looked down at the beautiful woman he held in his arms, his mother's quiet voice resonated in his mind.

Only after the rain comes the rainbow.

He couldn't have described his feelings any better. That's exactly what Cassie was. A beautiful, vibrant rainbow that promised hope, happiness, and a lifetime of sunshine. And Noah planned to make the most of every second.

Twenty-six

Six Weeks Later

By the time Cassie made it to Noah's, he and the girls were already hard at work on the banner. The garage door was open, and the three of them were sprawled across the dirty floor on their bellies, coloring and drawing. Noah had already outlined the word "WELCOME" in large block letters, and although they weren't the prettiest letters in the world, they looked okay—especially once the girls filled them in with bright colors and patterns.

Noah shifted positions to start on the H when Cassie placed her hand on his shoulder. "Um . . . Noah?"

"Yeah?" He craned his neck to look at her.

"I think you might be drawing the letters too big. The rest of the words aren't going to fit."

He glanced down the length of the banner. "Huh," he finally said. "You're probably right. I'll start drawing them smaller."

That was one way of fixing the problem, but it might be

better if "HOME" was written in small letters at the top with Emma, Georgia, and Maxwell at—

Too late, Noah was already making the adjustments himself, drawing every letter a little bit smaller than the last. How one person could be so talented in the art of woodworking and so bad at this (especially with an artist for a sister) was beyond Cassie. She had to bite her lip to keep from laughing at the finished message.

Maybe the girls' coloring job would help. Cassie crouched down opposite Noah, careful to only let her knees touch the floor, and pulled the cap off a pink marker. She began adding a few flowers to some of the letters in Georgia's name.

"That looks nice," said Noah. "But we need to hurry. She's going to be home any second."

Cassie quickly added a few more colorful details and helped the girls finish filling in the letters. Then they rolled up the banner and ran next door to hang it across Emma and Kevin's garage.

Right as they finished, Becky and Justin pulled up with a car full of pink and blue helium balloons.

"Cassie, you let Noah design the banner, didn't you?" was the first thing Becky said when she got out of the car.

"He'd already started by the time I got here, so there wasn't much I could do."

Noah took a few steps back, looking at the banner from afar. "What are you talking about? I think it looks great. It's, you know, little-kiddish."

"It's ridiculous," said Becky.

Adelynn frowned. "You don't like our coloring job, Aunt Becky?"

"Your coloring is perfect, as always. It's your father's drawing job that needs help."

Adelynn giggled and nodded.

"Traitor." Noah glared at his daughter, which only made her giggle harder.

The girls were covered in dust from the garage floor, so Cassie ushered them back to Noah's to change and wash up before Emma and Kevin arrived with Georgia and Maxwell. The girls ran to their room, and a few minutes later, a freshly changed Kajsa emerged, dragging the vacuum down the hallway.

"What are you doing?" Cassie asked. "We don't have time to vacuum right now."

"I want my hair in a ponytail." She plugged in the vacuum, handed Noah an elastic, then turned around.

Cassie had never been more confused. With deft movements, Noah wrapped the elastic around the handheld attachment of the vacuum before turning it on. Then he proceeded to suck his daughter's hair into the end.

"Noah!"

"What?" he said as he slid the elastic over an admittedly neat ponytail and shut off the vacuum.

"That's disgusting," said Cassie. "Do you know how many germs are inside that thing? Kajsa, sweetie, don't ever let your father do that again."

"But it's the only way he can do ponytails." Kajsa said as Adi emerged from her room, all changed. Together, they ran out the door, leaving Noah and Cassie alone in the hallway.

Cassie leaned her back against the wall and shook her head at Noah while she absentmindedly played with the relatively new diamond ring on her finger. It was small and understated, but she loved it. "I'm thinking that maybe we should move up the wedding date. Your girls obviously need a mother, and the sooner the better."

A smile appeared on his face as he took her into his arms. "Agreed. Next week sounds good."

"I was only joking."

"I wasn't."

Cassie laughed, looping her arms around his neck. "Maybe we can bump it to September instead of October."

"I think next week sounds better."

Cassie smiled and raised to her tiptoes, pressing her lips to his. She kissed him playfully at first, but when his large hands cradled her face, and his mouth worked its way across hers, the kiss changed into something stronger and more meaningful. Cassie clung to him, feeling everything—the warmth of his lips, the strength of his body, and the goodness of his heart. She felt it all.

Noah was a part of her now. He was in the walls of her basement, in the recesses of her mind, and in the crevices of her soul. This was what real love felt like. It wasn't superficial. It wasn't giddy. And it wasn't make-believe. It was something that reached deep inside her, molding and changing who she was and how she felt about the world, about people, about life. Cassie was no longer that forlorn and barren little geode, determined to take on the world by herself. She was the other half of a whole that was now brimming with crystals and sparkles and color.

Somewhere in the distance a horn honked and happy squeals followed. Noah's forehead came to rest against hers. "I think they're home. Want to go see your new niece and nephew?"

She smiled and nodded. And as he took her hand in his, Cassie knew joy.

Other books in the Meet Your Match Series . . .

Prejudice Meets Pride (Book1)

After years of pinching pennies and struggling to get through art school, Emma Makie's hard work finally pays off with the offer of a dream job. But when tragedy strikes, she has no choice but to make a cross-country move to Colorado Springs to take temporary custody of her two nieces. She has no money, no job prospects, and no idea how to be a mother to two little girls, but she isn't about to let that stop her. Nor is she about to accept the help of Kevin Grantham, her handsome neighbor, who seems to think she's incapable of doing anything on her own.

Prejudice Meets Pride is the story of a guy who thinks he has it all figured out and a girl who isn't afraid to show him that he doesn't. It's about learning what it means to trust, figuring out how to give and to take, and realizing that not everyone gets to pick the person they fall in love with. Sometimes, love picks them.

Stick in the Mud Meets Spontaneity (Book 3)

Home for the summer, Samantha Kinsey is ready to step into her role as pseudo-nanny for her two favorite charges. But when she realizes she'll be playing chauffeur more than play-mate, her summer outlook quickly turns from fun to bleak. That is, until she meets Colten McCoy—a genuine, hard-working cowboy, who's as set in his ways as he is handsome. Although he claims he doesn't need any spontaneity in his life, Sam's determined to help him find it. But she'll soon discover that cowboys are about as easy to change as wild mustangs.

Stick in the Mud Meets Spontaneity is about an adaptable girl and a not so adaptable guy. It's about learning to accept people for who they are and realizing that sometimes who they are is exactly who they should be.

If you're a fan of period romances, you may also enjoy my regency series . . .

If you'd like to be notified when future books are available, feel free to sign up for my New Release Newsletter at RachaelReneeAnderson.com.

Dear Reader,

Thanks so much for reading! I hope this story took you out of reality for awhile and into a world of escape and rejuvenation because everyone deserves that once in awhile.

If you're willing, I'd love a review from you on Goodreads or Amazon or wherever else you'd care to post one.

Or you can find me online at RachaelReneeAnderson.com.

Thanks again, and happy reading!

Rachael

Acknowledgements

First and foremost, I have to thank Karey White, for her listening ear, sound advice, friendship, and awesome editing skills. I owe you big-time.

Kathy Habel, thank you for your friendship, your marketing genius, encouragement, and for your honesty. I'm so grateful to know you.

Alison Blackburn, a million thanks for sharing your thoughts, insights, and brilliant mind with me. I'm so lucky to call you my friend.

Rebecca, thank you for your keen eye, words of encouragement, and friendship. You're amazing!

Karen P., thank you for being willing to proof my book. I'm so grateful for your help!

Jeff, bless you for helping, listening, encouraging, and for being the world's greatest husband, father, and friend. I love you.

And lastly, I have to thank my heavenly father, for loving me enough to challenge and bless me.

About Rachael Anderson

A *USA Today* bestselling author, Rachael Anderson is the author of six novels and three novellas. She's the mother of four and is pretty good at breaking up fights, or at least sending guilty parties to their rooms. She can't sing, doesn't dance, and despises tragedies. But she recently figured out how yeast works and can now make homemade bread, which she is really good at eating. You can read more about her and her books online at RachaelReneeAnderson.com.